We were surrounded by the spirits of the dead. . . .

"Look," I said, "we've got a problem. Is there anyone in this place we can talk to—anyone who's sort of in charge?"

The dead people glanced at each other. Finally one woman said, "No one is in charge here. But perhaps you could talk to Ivanoma."

"Who's that?" I asked.

"Ivanoma is a . . . well, it's sort of a counselor," said the woman.

"It?"

"Ivanoma is too—" The dead woman paused, then said slowly, "Well, it's too *much* to be a mere 'he' or 'she'."

"How do we get to this being?" asked Gaspar.

The woman looked at the silver cords that led back to our bodies in the world of the living. "I'm not sure you should go that far."

"The cords will hold," said Gaspar confidently.

I hoped he knew what he was talking about.

Look for these other Bruce Coville titles from Scholastic:

Bruce Coville's Book of Monsters
Bruce Coville's Book of Aliens
Bruce Coville's Book of Ghosts
Bruce Coville's Book of Nightmares
Bruce Coville's Book of Spine Tinglers
Bruce Coville's Book of Magic
Bruce Coville's Book of Monsters II
Bruce Coville's Book of Aliens II
Bruce Coville's Book of Ghosts II

and coming soon:

Bruce Coville's Book of Spine Tinglers II
Bruce Coville's Book of Magic II

BRUCE COVILLE'S BOOK OF

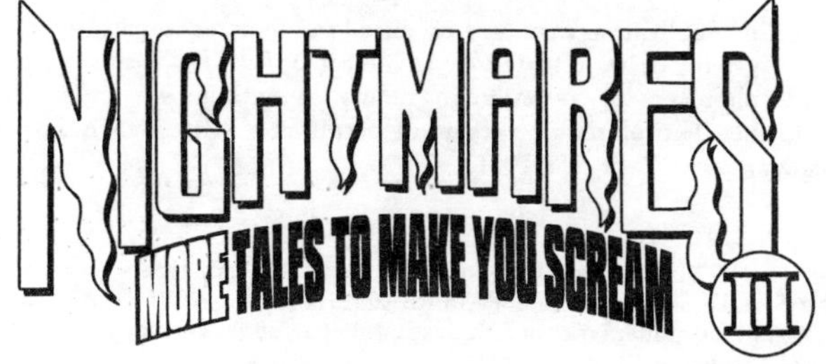

Compiled and edited by
Bruce Coville

Assisted by
Lisa Meltzer

Illustrated by
John Pierard

A GLC Book

AN
APPLE
PAPERBACK

SCHOLASTIC INC.
New York Toronto London Auckland Sydney

For Kitty,
who suffers for my sins.

ISBN 0-590-85295-7

12 11 10 9 8 7 6 5 4 3 2 1 7 8 9/9 0 2/0

Printed in the U.S.A. 40

First Scholastic printing, March 1997

CONTENTS

Contents

INTRODUCTION:

NIGHTMARE ALLEY

You sit up in bed, eyes wide, heart pounding, sweat streaming down your face.

Maybe you've even been screaming.

It can only mean one thing: You've been taking a walk down Nightmare Alley.

The alley is there every night, you know. Oh, some nights you manage to miss it, to walk right past as you make the long, dark trip from "Sweet dreams" to "Good morning!"

Some nights.

But other nights you're cruising through the darkness and for no reason at all you make a detour down Nightmare Alley and it all goes strange and scary. You dream of dark and nameless horrors waiting to swallow you up. Of being chased but not being able to run. Of being menaced but not being able to scream.

Fear cups you lovingly in its palm, then closes its cold fingers over your heart.

And the weird thing is, it all comes from

inside your own head. All that terror and tension, all that fright and fear, comes right out of your own brain.

What's even weirder is that we can't get enough of it. Menaced by nightmares when we sleep, we seek out fear while we're wide awake as well.

If you don't agree, why are you reading this book?

Well, don't worry, gentle reader. There's plenty of terror to go around. The writers who fill these pages know about nightmares, and have the appalling ability to conjure them up in broad daylight—to stir the pot of fear and dish up a steaming stew of terror to share with you.

Fortunately, it's only a book, and you're wide awake. You can close the pages and stop reading any time you want.

Or can you?

What if this is all a dream? What if when you decide to close the book, that's only a dream decision? What if the book is still there, waiting, and your brain is planning to open it again, whether you want it to or not?

What if you're dreaming right now?

What if you never wake up?

Heh heh heh.

Sweet dreams, my little dumplings.

WHEN EVIL WAKES (Part 4 of "The Monsters of Morley Manor")

Bruce Coville

What has happened so far:

My sister Sarah talked me into buying a weird wooden box at the house sale they had at Morley Manor the weekend before they were going to tear the old place down. Inside, we found five monster figurines—figurines that came to life when we got them wet! Before we knew it, Sarah and I were taking the monsters (Gaspar, Darlene, Albert, Marie, and Bob) back to Morley Manor so they could get big again.

As soon as we managed *that,* this weird alien called the Wentar showed up and said we had to get out of the house because some other aliens, the Flinduvians, were about to kick our butts. The Wentar led us through a "Starry

Door", which dropped us on another planet. There we learned that the Flinduvians were planning to kidnap Earth's ghosts to use in a weapon they had developed.

The Wentar took some of the monsters to spy on the aliens. The rest of us came back to warn the ghosts. Which explains what we were doing in the Land of the Dead . . .

I. Family Reunion

When Gramma Walker saw Grampa's ghost she started to cry. Not real tears, of course, since we weren't actually in our bodies. Still, you could tell she was crying by the way her shoulders shook.

Grampa looked . . . well, I can't tell you exactly how he looked, for two reasons. First, he had a lot of expressions moving across his face, including surprise, happiness, anger, and fear. Second, his face itself—which I knew very well—wasn't old, the way it used to be. But it wasn't young, either. It was as if all the ages he had ever been, all the faces he had worn through the years, had combined. His wrinkles were gone, but his eyes were old and wise.

He was also transparent. That didn't seem all that odd, since we were, too. But unlike us, he had no silver cord leading back to his body to hold him to the world of the living.

He stared at us for a long time. "You're not

dead," he said at last, his voice worried, puzzled, and relieved all at the same time.

"Well of course not, Horace," said Gramma matter-of-factly. I was surprised, at first, that she could hear him, since he had barely spoken above a whisper and she was nearly deaf. Then I realized her deafness was part of her physical body, and we had left those bodies behind when we entered the Land of the Dead.

"Then what are you doing here?" he asked. "And with the children! You shouldn't have come, Ethel!"

"We had to come, sir," said Gaspar.

Grampa turned toward him. "Gaspar?" he said slowly. "Gaspar Morley?" He squinted at our little group. "And Marie!" He said her name with something like a sob. "You're no older than when . . . but you're not dead, either! How can . . . Ethel, what's going on here? What are you doing here with *them?*"

"It's a long story," said Gaspar.

Grampa gestured to the misty void surrounding us, then said softly, "If there's one thing I've got, it's time."

"Actually, that may not be entirely true," Gaspar replied. "The reason we dared this journey is that we need to bring word to the dead that they are in danger."

"Dead is dead," said Grampa, sounding scornful.

"Really?" asked Gaspar. "It's true that you

are dead to the life you once knew. But though you no longer have your body, your *self* still exists. Now that is in danger as well."

Grampa snorted. "You sound like Reverend van Dyke. But don't worry. There's not much temptation around here. I don't think I'm in danger of any major sins at the moment."

Gaspar made a sound of frustration. "The danger is from outside, you old—" He cut himself off, and took a deep breath. Then he closed his eyes. I had a feeling he was counting to ten. Maybe higher. Finally he spoke again.

"There exists a great and powerful alien race, a group without pity or mercy. These people, the Flinduvians, have found a way to use the souls of Earth's dead to power a weapon they have created. If they should take you, sir, the result would be a second death. A permanent one. A death not of the body, but of the soul itself. Or perhaps worse. I do not really know what happens when a soul is used in this weapon of theirs. It could be far worse than mere oblivion."

Now Grampa did look frightened. "You're joking," he whispered.

"We did not come all the way to the Land of the Dead for the sake of a prank," said Gaspar sharply. "Now, is there someone you can take us to, a leader of any sort here?"

"I never thought I'd hear someone say, 'Take

me to your leader,' to a *ghost,*" whispered Sarah.

"I never thought I'd make a trip to the Land of the Dead," I replied softly.

Grampa's face got an odd expression, which I recognized as his thinking look. "I don't know if there's really a leader in this place. But I haven't been here all that long. Maybe there's something or someone I don't know about. Some souls greeted me when I arrived, helped calm me, keep me from being afraid. But since then I've been pretty much on my own."

"What have you been doing, Grampa?" I asked.

"Waiting. Thinking. Trying to let go." He glanced at my grandmother. "It's hard, Ethel. I don't want to let go. But that's what I'm supposed to do, I guess. I'm not really supposed to be here. None of us are. We're supposed to go on to . . . well, I don't exactly know. To something else. But I couldn't stop thinking about you."

He looked at Gaspar again, then said bitterly, "I didn't expect you to show up here with my old rival."

Gramma actually laughed. "Are you jealous, you old fool?" she asked, in her most loving voice.

"Jealous of the living," said Grampa.

Gramma stretched her hand toward him. "I suspect *that* would keep you here, if nothing else did, my love. You've got to let go, sweetheart. But not yet. Not until this nightmare is over."

She turned to me. "This is a nightmare, isn't it, Anthony? I mean, I am only dreaming, right?"

It would have been nice to tell her that was the case. But Gramma was fierce about the truth, and didn't like even the tiniest lies. Besides, who knew what else we were going to have to deal with before this was all over? If she thought this was a dream, it might lull her, make her less sharp, less ready to act. That was a luxury we couldn't afford.

So I shook my head. "It's no dream, Gramma."

She sighed. "Oh, I knew that. I was just sort of hoping . . . well, never mind. So what do we do now, Gaspar?"

Gaspar looked uncertain, which was unusual for him. "I guess we try to deliver our warning, then go home to see if the others have made it back."

Gramma turned back to Grampa. "Well, there it is, Horace. You have to help us deliver the warning."

She held out her arms and floated toward him.

Gaspar gestured to the rest of our group, and we turned to give the two old people, one living and one dead, a few minutes to themselves.

I used the time while Gramma and Grampa were playing snookie-face to get a better look at the place we were in.

There wasn't much to see, or so I thought at first. It was gray and misty, and seemed to roll on forever. Though it didn't have anything you could call landscape or scenery, I did get a sense of up and down, which was sort of weird. But we were all floating the same way up, as were the occasional dead people we saw drift by. So I figure the sense of up and down was real.

The ghosts—I guess that's what you would call them—pretty much ignored us. That was fine as far as I was concerned. The only time they looked our way was when Bob the were-dog growled at them, which he did until Marie shushed him. I guess they weren't used to seeing cocker spaniels in the Land of the Dead.

"I don't like it here," whispered Sarah, who was floating close to my side. "It feels cold."

Marie nodded "It is not pleasant. But remember, this is not where you will spend eternity. This is a place for those who have not moved on."

It's hard to have much of a sense of time in the Land of the Dead, so I don't really know how long it was before Gaspar made a noise in his throat to interrupt my grandparents, then said, "What would you suggest we do next, Horace?"

Grampa looked startled, as if he had forgotten the rest of us were there.

II. Ivanoma

Grampa looked at Gaspar for a long time. "I don't know," he said at last.

"Is there no one to contact?"

"Not that I can think of."

They went back and forth like that a couple more times until I finally got sick of it. I don't know what came over me. I had just had enough, I guess. Anyway, I threw my head back and yelled, "Hellllllp! I need to talk to someone!"

The others looked at me as if I had just farted in church, which I guess I can understand. Something about the Land of the Dead seemed to demand that you should be hushed and quiet.

But hushed and quiet wasn't getting us anywhere.

The silence that followed my outburst was broken when Marie started to laugh.

It was a rich, beautiful sound.

And it was like bait.

Within moments, we were surrounded by spirits of the dead, dozens of translucent men and women (and a few children), all staring at

Marie with a look I can only describe as *hunger.*

"Laughter is something you don't hear much of in these parts," explained Grampa softly.

Marie looked nervous, but I figured this was our big chance. "Look," I said, "we've got a problem. Is there anyone in this place we can talk to—anyone who's sort of in charge?"

The dead people glanced at each other. Finally one of the women said, "No one is in charge here. But perhaps you could talk to Ivanoma."

"Who's that?" I asked. I was a little surprised that the grownups were letting me carry the conversation, but I guess they figured I had started it and unless I made some mistake they'd let me keep it going.

"Ivanoma is a . . . well, it's sort of a counselor," said the woman.

"It?" I asked.

"Ivanoma is too—" The dead woman paused, then said slowly, "Well, it's too *much* to be a mere 'he' or 'she'."

The others surrounding us murmured in agreement.

"Don't look at me," said Grampa, when we all turned in his direction. "I never heard of this Ivanoma, whatever it is."

"How do we get to this being?" asked Gaspar.

The woman looked at our silver cords. "I'm not sure you should go that far," she said.

That made me nervous. If there was one thing I didn't want to do, it was break the connection that held me to my body.

"The cords will hold," said Gaspar confidently.

I hoped he knew what he was talking about.

"Then follow me," said the woman.

To travel in the Land of the Dead is strange. At first, I thought there was little to mark the passing of distance, since everything looks the same. But as we moved on, I began to see vague hints of the world of the living. It was little more than shapes in the mist, different shades and tones in the gray. But it was very real. I realized we were moving *very* fast. I began to worry about the silver cords.

Suddenly we plunged downward.

Below us stretched a great lake of ice. Chained flat on its back in the center of the lake was the most beautiful creature I had ever seen. The being was enormous, maybe a hundred feet tall. Vast, perfectly formed wings stretched from its shoulders across the clear ice.

The being—I assumed it was Ivanoma—lay very still, staring upward into the mist and the darkness. Clusters of the dead surrounded it, leaning against its sides, floating around its huge and magnificent head, resting on its breast.

From its eyes flowed a neverending stream of tears.

Some of the dead were bathing in them.

I felt fear, and awe, and pity, as we floated toward the creature.

Suddenly it blinked and lifted its head. Then it raised one vast and shapely arm, the chains that held it to the ice separating as if they were made of nothing but mist, though they had looked more solid than steel just a moment earlier.

"Why have the living come to the Land of the Dead?" it asked, in a whisper that had as many tones, as much music, as a choir.

As it spoke, it held out its hand in a clear invitation for us to land upon it.

So we did. Though our bodies were not really there—though we were, in truth, lighter than air—I could see the being flinch when we touched it. The palm of its hand sank as if a great weight had just been dropped into it.

We stood in the center of the being's hand, and it lowered us, to hold us right before its eyes.

Its eyes.

If I had a hundred years I couldn't tell you what it was like to look into those eyes, except to say that it was like taking a bath in pain and beauty, and I was afraid I might never be

able to look at the regular world, at anything else, again.

My mother told me once that the memory of pain fades. She said if it didn't, women would never have more than one baby.

I think it must be true for other things as well, things like beauty, and love. If the memory of gazing into those eyes—each of which was a yard wide and several thousand miles deep—had not faded I doubt I could move in the world today. I would only sit and remember.

For a long time none of us spoke. Finally it was me, me the mouthy one, who asked, "Are you Ivanoma?"

It nodded.

"Are you an angel?"

It nodded again.

"Why are you here? Why are you so sad?"

None of this was what we had come to say. But it was all that I could think of.

"I made a mistake once," whispered the angel, in a voice that would have made Mozart weep with envy because he could never write music that beautiful. "I chose the wrong side in an ancient war. I am paying for my sin."

But your chains don't hold you," I said, thinking of how it had lifted its hand to receive us.

Ivanoma actually smiled. I thought that I

would die of joy on the spot. "My chains are of my own making, and I can break them at any time. I *choose* to be here, to console the dead, to offer them help, and guidance, and love, when they are ready to receive it."

I saw Gramma nudge Grampa, as if to say, "You should have taken advantage of this, you old fool."

"The dead need your help now," I said.

Ivanoma raised a single eyebrow. The gesture was like a sunrise.

Quickly, I told the angel what we knew about the Flinduvians.

Its frown nearly killed me.

"I know this to be true," it whispered in a voice that throbbed with pain, as if it held the weight of ten thousand years of human misery. "I have sensed five times in the last moments—you must understand, moments are different to me than they are to you—I have sensed five times someone being wrenched from the Land of the Dead, heard a cry of terror, felt a stab of fear different from the fear I feel when they enter here. I did not know what it meant."

"Can you help?" I cried.

"I can warn the dead," Ivanoma replied.

"Surely you can do more than that," I said urgently. "You are so strong, so powerful."

"I am bound," replied Ivanoma.

"But you can break the chains!"

"I have promised not to."

And that was all it would say. It was all we had come for, really. We wanted to warn the dead. Ivanoma said it would do that for us. Our mission was accomplished. But still . . .

"Come," whispered Gaspar. "It's time for us to leave."

He might as well have said it was time to rip my heart out of my chest and drop it, still beating, into the dog's dish.

"Leave?" I cried. "We can't leave!"

"You must," whispered Ivanoma. "The living do not belong here. It was brave of you to come, but you must go back where you belong. Let me warn the dead. You must tend to the living."

The angel closed its eyes and lay its head back against the frozen lake.

It was like being released from a trap you didn't know was holding you. I could never have left the Land of the Dead as long as I was looking into those eyes. Now I was free to go.

And I did go, almost instantly, for in the space of less than a heartbeat we were back in our bodies, back in the world of the living.

It was clear that Ivanoma had hurried us on our way.

It was also soon clear that the angel had made another mistake.

III. Martin

When I opened my eyes, I saw nothing but deep blackness. For a minute I feared I hadn't made it back after all. Then I remembered we had left our bodies in a sub-sub-basement of Morley Manor, and that the place was completely dark.

I heard Sarah stirring beside me. "Anthony?" she whispered. "Are you there?"

"I'm here," I said quietly.

"Did all that really happen?"

"I think so."

"It was real," said Gaspar. I heard him fumbling around. He struck a match. Even though it was a tiny flame, in the darkness the sudden flare seemed horribly bright. As I blinked against it I saw that Marie was sitting up, brushing herself off. Bob was still lying on his side, twitching and whining.

Gramma was not moving at all.

I scrambled to my feet to see if she was okay. As I did, I heard a familiar voice cry, *Ethel! Ethel, are you all right?* I stopped dead, so to speak.

"Grampa?" I said softly. "Grampa, is that you?"

Uh-huh. He sounded subdued, embarrassed almost.

"Where are you?"

I heard Gaspar curse as the match's flame

reached his fingertips. He dropped it. We were in darkness again.

"Anthony, who are you talking to?" asked Sarah.

Gramma groaned.

Thank goodness she's alive! said Grampa.

"Where are you?" I shouted.

"Right here," said Sarah.

"Not you," I snapped. "Grampa!"

I'm right here, too, said Grampa.

Suddenly I realized what he meant. Horrified, I grabbed the sides of my head and shouted, "What are you doing in there?"

He sighed. *I'm sorry, Anthony. When Ivanoma sent the group back, he—I mean* it*—accidentally made it possible for me to—well, to sort of hitch a ride with you. I landed in your body.*

"You *what?*"

Grampa sighed. *I've missed your grandmother so much, Anthony. Having been so close to her, seen her again, I just couldn't let go.*

"But this is—"

I was interrupted by someone shaking me. "Anthony!" said Gaspar sharply. "Are you all right?"

I realized that though I had been talking to Grampa out loud, his answers had all been inside my head. I must have sounded as if I was totally wacked.

Don't tell them I'm here! said Grampa urgently.

"What?"

Your grandmother won't like it. She'll be mad. Please, Anthony—I'll leave as soon as I can.

I didn't say anything for a minute.

PLEASE!

I sighed. Grampa had always been good to me. What was I going to do? Send him back to the Land of the Dead?

We'll talk about this later, I thought, hoping he would understand me if I spoke only in my head.

Thanks, Anthony. You're a pal.

Well, obviously he could understand my thoughts. Out loud I said, "Sorry, Gaspar. Guess I was woozy from the trip."

"Speak up, Anthony," said a voice from below me.

"Gramma!" I cried. "You're all right!"

"Well, mostly," she said. "My hearing is gone again. Too bad about that. No surprise, though."

She started to stand up. *Help her!* said Grampa, but Gaspar beat me to it. I could sense Grampa's annoyance.

"Well," said Gramma, once she was on her feet again. "I must say I never expected anything like this when I told your parents I would watch you for the weekend." Her voice was kind of shaky.

"We'd better get upstairs," said Gaspar. He sounded a little shaky too, which made me nervous. "I wonder when the others will get back."

What he didn't say, but I suspected was on his mind, was that it wasn't just a question of *when* the others would get back.

It was a question of *if*.

What would happen if they were caught in Flinduvia?

Maybe that was why he was shaky. After all, this was his family we were talking about.

As it turned out, the return of the others was one thing we *didn't* have to worry about. When we got upstairs—all the way upstairs, to the lab—we found Albert, Darlene, and the Wentar waiting for us.

With them was a skinny, dark-haired boy, not much older than me. He was dressed in a one-piece outfit that looked as if someone had made a pair of coveralls out of blue aluminum foil.

"Martin!" cried Gaspar in astonishment.

"Martin?" echoed Sarah, Gramma, and I all at the same time. (Actually, Grampa said it too, but I was the only one who could hear him.)

"But he's just a kid!" I said.

"Of course he's still a youngster," said the Wentar, who was standing behind the boy, looking gloomy as usual. "He's been in suspended animation for nearly a century!"

Martin was staring up at Gaspar with an expression that seemed half fearful, half hungry. Suddenly I realized how strange it must be for this boy to see his twin—who had looked just like him from the time they had both been born—as a grown man, while he was still a boy.

It was a good thing Gaspar had at least gotten rid of his lizard head! (Something Darlene and Albert had seemed only moderately surprised to notice.)

Martin said something. The words were in a foreign language. That was a surprise, but only because I was being sort of stupid. Of course he spoke a foreign language. The Flinduvians had kidnapped him when he was still a kid living in Transylvania and they had had him in suspended animation ever since. What did I think he would speak? Basic American?

The second, and much bigger, surprise came when Gaspar answered in the same language and I could understand it!

I blinked and looked at Sarah. She appeared to be as startled as I was. Then she smiled. "The spell!" she exclaimed. "It's still working!"

Duh! That explained it, of course. When we

were on the planet of the frog-critters (I never did learn the official name for the place) the Wentar had cast a translation spell on us so that we could understand the frog guys. Clearly the spell had been more effective than we had realized.

What Gaspar said was, "So, the big brother is now the little brother, and the little the big. Welcome back to the world we know, Martin."

Martin's face quavered. I thought for a moment he was going to cry. But then he got control of himself. It was as if his face froze in place.

I had enough sense of Gaspar by now to realize that normally he would try to comfort a kid who was feeling as bad as Martin seemed to. But Martin wasn't just any kid. Not only was he Gaspar's twin brother, he was—or had been—the just-barely *older* brother. And from what Gaspar had told us, Martin had always taken advantage of the fact. Not only that, during the thirty years that passed between the time Martin fell into Flinduvia and the time that his replacement clone shrank and froze Gaspar and the others, the family had lived with the belief that the clone was the real Martin.

What a mess! No wonder they all seemed to have feelings that were, to say the least, confused. I tried to imagine what it would be like for me to go to sleep some night, and wake up to find my little sister was now a forty-year-old woman. The idea gave me the willies, and I figured it would have been even weirder if she had been my twin. And weirder still if I had first been rescued from an alien planet and dragged back to a foreign country by someone like the Wentar.

No wonder poor Martin looked like he wanted to cry!

It was Darlene who broke the moment. She went to Martin and put her arms around him. "Poor little brother," she whispered.

This gesture might have been more comforting to Martin if she had not shown her vampire fangs while she spoke. Looking startled, he pulled away from her. "Leave me alone!" he shouted.

Then he put his face in his hands and began to sob.

Her own lips quivering, Darlene dropped her hands to her sides and stepped back. At the same time Gaspar went to stand beside Martin. He said nothing, only put one hand gently on his shoulder.

Martin pushed away and bolted for the door.

Albert and I both started after him. Before we had taken two steps the Wentar raised his hand and made a weird gesture.

Martin slumped to the floor.

Bob threw back his head and howled.

"What have you done?" cried Marie.

"It is merely a spell of sleep," said the Wentar sharply. "He will rest in comfort while we talk. And we must talk, for there is a great deal to say, and not much time to say it."

Who's the tall, bossy guy? asked Grampa.

It's a long story, I thought back.

That's all right. I think I can figure it out on my own if I just look around in here a bit.

I blinked and shook my head. *Hey! No fair poking around in my head without my permission!*

It's all right, Anthony. Believe me, once you're dead, a lot of stuff you used to take seriously isn't really all that important. For example, I already stumbled across a memory that told me it was you who broke that cellar window three years ago. I would have been mad at the time. Now—eh, there's more important stuff to worry about.

I was trying to concentrate on what was going on with Gaspar and the monsters. But Grampa said something else then that has stayed in my head ever since. I didn't really listen at the time, so I suspect he etched it in my brain somehow, leaving it as a little present for me.

I can still hear him say it, as if he was inside my head even now, instead of—

Well, instead of where he is.

Anthony, all your life people are going to tell you to stop and smell the roses. But they won't usually tell you why. So let me give you one good reason, the one I learned too late. There are no gardens in the Land of the Dead. You have to embrace life now, Anthony—now while you're still part of it. Grab it to you. See it, feel it, hold it, love it. Don't let it pass you by, boy. Don't shut yourself off from it. Because the truth is, you never know what moment is going to be your last, what scent, what sound, what smell will be the last one you experience. Make it good. Make it real.

Probably pretty good advice, coming from a dead man. But I didn't answer him then, mostly because the Wentar recaptured my attention by saying, "Martin has already given us some vital information—namely, why the Flinduvians want Earth's dead."

"And just why is that?" asked Gaspar.

"They intend to use them to reanimate their own dead."

"Well that's silly," said Darlene. "If they can do that, why don't they just use the souls of their own dead?"

The Wentar made a sniffing sound. "A more cynical being than I might say it is because Flinduvians have no souls. Like most nice, simple answers, it is not accurate. The real reason is more complicated."

He glanced over at Martin, as if to make sure he was still asleep, and then continued. "Though the Starry Doors provide a wonderful way to travel from world to world, that very ease of transport carries with it the possibility of evil."

"Why?" I asked.

"Because if it were unlimited it would allow renegade planets to launch massive invasions of other worlds without warning. Of course, we don't have many planets like that, since we carefully screen worlds before we allow them access to the doors. Even so, sometimes mistakes . . . happen."

"Like the Flinduvians?" asked Gaspar.

"Precisely," said the Wentar. "Allowing them into the Coalition of Civilized Worlds was one of our few mistakes, and one of our worst. They are subdued now, and have been for some time. But it is a world where a great evil lies sleeping. It would not take much to waken it, for the Flinduvians have a lust for conquest. To guard against such peoples using the doors improperly, those who designed them specified that no more than ten members of a species can pass through a specific gate on any given day."

"I still don't understand what this has to do with our ghosts," I said.

"I'll be glad to explain," hissed a voice from behind me.

I turned, then screamed.

The Flinduvians had arrived.

When Evil Wakes

IV. The Flinduvian Plan

The first time I saw a Flinduvian, it had been tearing its way through a barrier to our world. I had gotten only a peek at it, because just as it was breaking through we had fled through a Starry Door.

Though that brief sight had not been encouraging, the reality turned out to be even worse than I expected.

To begin with, they were big, between six and eight feet tall. Of course, Gaspar and the Wentar were tall, too. But they didn't have biceps like basketballs, and thighs as big around as my waist. We're not talking *fat* thighs, either. I could see that they were solid muscle (or whatever Flinduvians have) because the aliens' uniforms consisted of nothing more than tight-fitting shorts, broad silver armbands, and chest harnesses to hold weapons and ammunition. They didn't even wear shoes, which you would think would be a basic item for warrior types. At least, you would think that if you hadn't seen a Flinduvian's foot, which is sort of like a horse's hoof made long and flexible.

Their fingers were even more flexible, since they weren't really fingers but scale-covered tentacles. What really gave me the creeps was that the tentacles were of different lengths and thicknesses. I figured this meant they had specialized uses . . . something I decided not to think about too much.

The Flinduvian's muscles weren't the only things that bulged. They also had bulging snouts and eyes.

Mom has always taught me not to judge people by their looks, but I was having a hard time following that advice right then. The Flinduvians looked big, mean, and nasty, and my gut feeling was that they probably acted the same way.

There were ten of them, and they pretty much filled the room.

The guy at the front, who I assumed was their leader, smiled.

I wished he hadn't. Not because of the two rows of silvery fangs, though they were bad enough. No, it was the black, snaky tongue flickering out of his mouth that really got to me. It was far more horrible and frightening than Gaspar's had been, probably because it had two big holes in the end of it—holes that opened and closed like sniffing nostrils.

"The plan is simple," he said, in a voice that was deep and hissy, but also surprisingly musical. "While no more than ten members of a species may pass through a gate, that restriction applies only to the living. We can transport as many *corpses* as we wish. Once we have them here, we can inject the spirits of Earth's dead, and bring them back to life."

"What good will that do you?" asked Gaspar. "You can't expect Earth's dead to fight on your behalf."

"They'll have no choice," said the Flinduvian cheerfully. "All we need is their life force to animate the bodies. Once we install it, their actions will be completely under our control."

"And where are you going to get an army's worth of corpses?" asked Gaspar.

The alien smiled again. "No Flinduvian hesitates to die in the service of his planet. When the call goes out for bodies our biggest problem will be sorting through the many volunteers eager to earn a spot in warrior heaven. Such a death is a great honor, a privilege."

"If you can put a soul into a body, why don't you just reinsert the being who was there to begin with?" asked Darlene.

The leader sneered. "Once a being has actually died, reinstalling its soul into a body can give it power and movement, but not genuine life. They will be mere zombies." (He didn't actually use the word "zombie," of course, since he was speaking in Flinduvian. But that was the sense of it.) "To be trapped in such a thing is not a proper fate for the soul of a Flinduvian hero. That's why it was such a great boost to our plans when we captured young Martin there. By studying him we eventually discovered what an absurdly strong connection to life the ghosts of this miserable, long-ignored little planet of yours possess—strong enough to make them cling even to an alien body. It makes them perfect for our uses."

He threw back his head and laughed. At least, I think it was a laugh. The actual sound was sort of a cross between a chainsaw and a werewolf gargling. "Now, at last, Flinduvia will rouse from her slumber! Now we wake—and the galaxy trembles!"

I heard a groan, and turned to see Martin push himself to a kneeling position. Darlene started toward him.

"Don't move!" snapped the Flinduvian.

Martin looked up at the sound of his voice. "Oh, it's you! It's about time. I was wondering when you were going to get here."

"Martin, what are you talking about?" cried Gaspar.

"Be quiet, you fool," snapped the boy. "Why do you think I let the Wentar bring me back here? Does the word 'bait' mean anything to you?"

Darlene started to cry. Gramma put an arm around her shoulder.

That's my Ethel, thought Grampa. *Always worried about others.*

Though he didn't say anything else, I caught a note of terror running beneath his thoughts. He was right to be terrified. The very moment he sent those words to me, one of the Flinduvian's armbands began to beep.

The leader of the group smiled, and his tongue flicked out. "Well," he said happily. "It looks as if we have a ghost near us right now. Might as well collect it while we have the chance. Who knows when it will prove to be useful?"

The Flinduvian behind him, the one with the beeping armband, turned in a slow circle. When he was facing in my direction, the armband began to beep more loudly. His blue face creased in one of those horrible tongue-flicking smiles, and he stepped toward me.

The beeping increased.

The alien looked puzzled. "Are you harboring one of the dead, boy?"

I shook my head, trying to look both innocent and stupid.

It did no good. The alien raised his hand. He was holding something shaped like a gun, except that it had a big, clear chamber at the back of it.

He pointed it at my head, then pulled the trigger.

TO BE CONTINUED IN
BRUCE COVILLE'S BOOK OF SPINE TINGLERS II

On the hill beside our house we had a place to bury our pets. But we always planted our pumpkins somewhere else . . .

CIRCLE OF LIFE

Michael and Rozalyn Mansfield

Corey walked silently through the field behind the house that he shared with his father. Tears slid down his cheeks as he cradled the unmoving form of his dog, Shags, wrapped in the dog's favorite blanket. He came to a spot beneath a great oak tree. Neat piles of moss-covered stones were scattered through it. The stones marked the graves of his father's boyhood pets, animals brought home from the woods and pond. Corey hoisted the dog and walked among them until he came to a central spot. He laid Shags down. Then he picked up the shovel he'd set down earlier and began to dig.

His mind was filled with memories of other sun-filled summer afternoons, when Shags would dart off, following his nose. Corey would follow the dog through the tall hot grass, past leaping squirrels and jackrabbits, into the shadow-dappled woods. Dark smells of decaying leaves and swampy mold would draw Shags toward the pond, through bushes spotted with tiny narrow lizards, green as the summer leaves they sat on. Shags would poke his nose in every bush, sniffing for frogs.

It always seemed a surprise to Shags when a bullfrog would spring out, squawking, to splash into the water. Eager for a swim, boy and dog would leap after, plunging through the rippling surface to the icy-cold, dim green depths. At last they'd come up, gasping and shivering, leaving the frog to swim away. Corey would laugh to see Shags, his fur covered with algae and pond weed, looking greener than the frogs he'd chased.

Later they'd wander home, to sit on the back porch as the glare of day faded into evening, fireflies twinkling across the field. Snuggled against him, Shags would shift and wriggle, ears popping up at forest sounds Corey could barely hear. Shags had shared evenings with Corey for all of the boy's eleven years, for the dog had been part of the family even longer than he had. Corey would laugh at his father's jokes about how when Corey was a baby Shags had taught him how to eat solid food, accounting for the boy's table manners from then on.

When Corey's mother died in a car accident when he was eight, Shags had been there to comfort him, though he could not take away the pain. Corey had felt Shags would always be there.

But last night was different. Shags hadn't seemed to hear the night sounds. He had wheezed and wobbled stiffly, shivering against Corey in the steamy evening, before sticking his warm nose into the boy's side. It had been happening more and more lately. Corey's dad said the dog was just getting old. Corey had stroked the long black and white fur as Shags, whining softly, looked up lovingly. At last the dog sank his head into Corey's lap and slipped into a troubled sleep. Corey carried him into his bedroom and lay down beside the dog's blanket with him. Through the night Corey anxiously stroked the small huddled form. But in the morning, Shags was gone.

Now there was only the dog's body on the ground and the hole Corey was digging to put it into. The heavy weight in his stomach, the tightness in his throat, would not go away. At the sound of footsteps he looked up to see his father coming toward the old oak. Frowning, Corey thrust the shovel in the hole and dug deeper.

"It doesn't seem any easier just because Shags was old, does it?" asked his dad.

"No," said Corey, swallowing.

"He did have a wonderful long life with you."

"Why'd it have to end?" asked Corey bitterly.

His father sighed. "Everything dies sooner or later, Corey." He bent down to straighten a stone on one of the piles. "This is where I buried my pet owl. He stayed with me when he could have gone. I felt the way you do now when he finally couldn't stay any longer."

Corey didn't answer right away. He finished digging the hole, then lowered Shags into the ground. "Nobody's ever felt the way I do, Dad," he said. "You just don't understand. He's *always* been with me—"

Corey stopped, tears choking him. "Now he'll never—I can't be without him, not Mom and him, too—"

Corey's father hugged him clumsily. "In a way he's still here, you know. I know it's not the same, but he'll become part of this field, making plants grow, and making new life. It's all a cycle. Nothing is ever really lost. Haven't you ever noticed how the flowers in this part of the field grow the fastest and best?"

Corey nodded, thinking about what his father had just said. As he finished the grave, an idea began to form, a way to bring Shags back into his life.

By the next day the idea had become a plan. He carried a paper sack, rustling with pumpkin seeds, to the old oak. Every summer Corey grew his own pumpkins for Halloween. He saved the seeds from the best ones, trying to grow bigger and better ones. This year he would grow the best one of all.

He knelt and dug a hole just above the spot where Shags lay. Opening the bag, he shook the seeds into his hand. He looked at them carefully and felt them for firmness. At last he selected one, looked at it for a long moment, and then made a small hole with his hands and put it in the ground. "There you stay," he said importantly, "and grow, and the cycle will go on." He covered it with dirt, patted it down, and gathered several rocks to place in a circle around the seed.

Through the summer days Corey played games of tag across the fields with friends and climbed trees as high as the branches would hold him. Each morning he mixed a shovelful of horse manure from the neighbors' farm in a bucket of water, then brought it to the plant and poured the mixture around the roots. It grew into a luxuriant vine, spotted with huge orange blossoms. On four or five flowers, pumpkins began to grow. One morning Corey got up at dawn to inspect them. He looked at all of the baseball-size green balls swelling behind the withered flower petals.

"It has to be the right one," he told himself, "just one pumpkin to grow big and carry Shags back to me. Just the right pumpkin."

He left the largest and roundest one. The others he cut off the vine with his pocketknife.

Summer waned, and school started again. Halloween approached. Corey kept watch over his pumpkin, going to it in the dewy morning, coming back to sit by it with his homework in the cool of the evening. Afterward he would stay and tell it stories about Shags.

The pumpkin grew huge and round and orange, glowing in the dusk. It was larger than Corey had dared hope; it was like a beautiful swelling womb, cradling Shags's spirit within. "He's there, I know he's there," Corey whispered to himself.

Corey dreamed he saw the pumpkin's roots spread through the ground in shining pathways, gently absorbing what was left of Shags's body. In the cradling pumpkin, it grew once more into the living dog Corey loved. Just before the boy awoke from his dream, he saw the pumpkin split open and Shags push through to bound into his arms.

On Halloween, Corey took his father to see the pumpkin. "Look how big it is, Dad."

"It's the best one you're ever grown," his father agreed. "If you save the seeds, you can plant a new one for Shags next year."

"Sure, Dad," said Corey absently.

"And maybe by then you'll be ready to love a new pup."

Corey gave him a strange smile. "I love Shags, Dad. *He's* my dog. *You're* not ready to love a new mom for me."

"I—it's not the same, Corey," his father said.

"To me it is," Corey told him.

His father winced and turned away. Corey watched him walk back to the house alone, then turned back to the pumpkin. It seemed even bigger tonight than it had that morning. The full moon had risen, glowing golden in the clear evening, like another pumpkin in the sky. Its light sparkled across the pumpkin's surface.

Suddenly Corey took an eager step forward. Something was happening! The pumpkin was shifting, starting to swell and contract, gently at first, then more intensely. After his first step Corey stopped, not making a sound, fear and hope both holding him back. The pumpkin rippled. A crack opened in its side.

Corey held his breath as a paw started to push through, and the gleam of a loving brown eye, and part of a moist black nose. He heard his heart pounding, a great beat of joy. The crack split wider.

Then the head pushed through farther—and a paw, a wing, a long snakey tentacle. The boy gasped. The brown dog eye looked at him; on its other side a golden frog eye glowed and stared. Frog, owl, bat, snake, cat, Shags, all in a hideous jumble. The creature surged out of the pumpkin and came at him, running, slithering, flying—

Corey shrank back. A strange whine came from the creature's mouth, and its dog eye

looked at him with overwhelming devotion. Corey trembled as it approached him, shaking and straining. It stopped when it reached him, shuddering, as if all the other animals of its makeup were battling with Shags. The frog eye blinked and the creature's mouth writhed. Then it sniffed Corey's hand. A strange, misshapen tongue came out of its mouth and licked him. The creature shuddered again, and then turned toward the woods. Flapping, slithering, hopping, it disappeared into the night.

Corey sank to his knees, sobbing. He hadn't realized how far pumpkin roots could grow.

Through that long night, while other kids were ringing doorbells and calling "Trick or Treat!", Corey stayed in the corner of the field, staring into the darkness. He listened, straining his ears, trying to identify rustles, squeaks, slithers. And wondered. And shivered.

I thought Ann Manheimer was perfectly normal when I first met her. But that was before she sent me this story.

THE DOLLHOUSE

Ann S. Manheimer

September 10:

It was really weird this morning with the ambulance screaming to a stop next door and red and blue lights flying everywhere. They found both of them, old Jake and Angela Fowler, there in their bed. Mom says it's a great way to go, but I think it's creepy, like everything else about those old folks.

Like the way old Mrs. Fowler hasn't been seen around for a week or two, but here she turns up dead, right next to the old man.

Like the way Mr. Fowler talked to his roses and petted them and treated them as if they were kids, and then yelled at all the real kids around him if anyone let a ball or something even just get close to his stupid flowers.

Like how they always stared at me, with

their drippy eyes through heavy bottle-lens glasses, and how they always called me "Nina" instead of my real name, "Lina," and how they were always trying to talk to me and never screamed at me like they did all the other kids, even my little sister, Creepy Charlie herself. Old Mr. Fowler was right there at our fence like always yesterday, watering his roses, his mouth moving up and down in a dribbly, quivering sort of way, staring up at my window so I could've sworn he saw me, but of course, how could he with my lights off and through the screen and everything?

Mom says it's because I remind them of their dead daughter, Nadine. She had dark hair, like mine, and was about my age when she died. That was years and years ago, long before we moved into the big house next to theirs, when Mom was still a kid. Mom's seen pictures, though, and she says she looked a little like me.

It's kind of sad, but sometimes I think maybe she just checked out on purpose because of it being such a nightmare having the Fowlers for parents, with the way they must have looked at her all the time as if she were a bug under a microscope. They were definitely not the kindly old neighborhood couple. I don't think Mrs. Fowler ever tasted a chocolate chip cookie, much less baked one.

Even Mom didn't like them, but she won't admit it. They were our landlords. Mom says they moved to the little house when Nadine got polio and couldn't climb the stairs in ours anymore. She says they're sad, they had hard lives. Well, Mom's had a hard life, too, with Daddy taking off when Charlie was just a baby and her job and all, but she doesn't go around scaring little kids and poisoning cats. Poor Fluffy, from across the street, just because she poked her little head around those stupid roses where they put the poison.

A man in a blue suit came and looked through their house. Mom says he's their lawyer. He asked Mom if she knew any of the Fowlers' relatives. Of course we don't, and Mom said so. He said he'd be back and drove away in this cool little red car.

I'm kind of glad I have to keep this journal for Mr. Cayou's English class after all. It helps for stuff like this, and when I don't want to do boring pre-algebra homework.

Still, I can't believe they're really dead. They were there, and now it's like they never were, except for the stuff they left behind.

Lina

September 11:

The red car was parked in front again when I got home from school today, and I could see the same blue suit through the Fowlers' front window. You'd think, being a lawyer and all, he'd be able to buy more clothes.

Then I noticed someone's been messing with the roses. A couple of plants are gone, dirt's all thrown around. In the middle are some dried flowers that somebody stuck in pots. At least when the Fowlers were there, the place always looked neat, that's the one good thing you could say about them.

Mr. Fowler had been doing stuff with his roses, not just growing them. He was some kind of professor. He retired early because of Nadine's dying, but he was still doing experiments or something. I mean, smart and nice really are different.

It had something to do with shaping the roses. He tried to tell me about it once, when he started talking to me like he always did if he was outside when I got home. I was polite because of what Mom said about their being sad and all, so when he started talking to me about stuff like heat exchange and dimensions, I pretended I was interested.

He said if you can catch something as it's turning, just about to go into a different dimension, you can figure its pattern and, I think he said, "redirect its heat," but you have to have something similar to make an exchange with. The only part I understood was about dimensions, so I asked if he meant width and depth, like I learned in science. Then he said something so weird, I still remember his exact words:

"There are other dimensions, ones you won't

learn about in science, Nina. There's the other reality. Like dreams. Or nightmares."

I got chills all over when he said that, and I started backing away. I mean, I didn't even want to tell him not to call me Nina, he sounded so weird. But then he said he was talking about fractals, and I felt better. Ms. Thomas talked about fractals in pre-algebra; they're just pictures you can make from equations. Old Fowler looked so pleased when I said that, I thought he'd drool all over himself. Then he started using words like *iteration* and *algorithms.* I got away quick after that.

Lina

September 14:

I can't believe they gave the dollhouse to Creepy Charlie! I mean, I thought the Fowlers were the only ones she hadn't fooled into thinking she's so cute with her blond curls and stuff. Grown-ups are always saying how she looks just like that old child actress, Shirley Temple, and going all gaga over her. Except the Fowlers. They never paid her any attention. Only me.

Don't get me wrong. It's not like *I* want anything from those two, especially not a dumb toy I'm way too old for. But you'd think, with the way they talked to *me* and stared at *me* all the time, they would've given it to *me.*

I was doing pre-algebra when the gardener

brought it over, so I haven't seen it yet. I didn't even see the lawyer this time, though his car's still out front, but I did see the back of the gardener. He's old, with white hair. Mom said the lawyer hired him to take care of the house while they get it ready to sell. I wonder what they'll do with our house, if we'll have to move.

Anyway, this gardener dropped off a letter from the lawyer that the Fowlers wanted Charlie to have the dollhouse because Mr. Fowler built it for their daughter and they didn't have anybody else to give it to. So I wonder what that makes me, chopped liver or something?

Lina

September 15:

One thing you can say for that stupid dollhouse—it keeps the Creep out of my hair. All she's done since she got it is stay in her room and play with it. I can hear the funny voices she uses through the wall.

I finally got to see it, but I had to ask Charlie if I could—it's not like she was all rushing in to show it off like usual. It seemed like she didn't want to show me, but she couldn't think of a reason not to, and with Mom standing right there, I guess she had to. She opened her door to let me look at it.

It's really big. It takes up a whole corner in Charlie's room. It's got lots of details, too, with windows and stairs and everything. There are even a couple of tiny rosebushes on the outside, that look incredibly like the Fowlers', instead of the usual dollhouse dried, potted flowers. What's weird is how nobody else notices how it looks exactly like our house. Charlie didn't say anything when I said so. When I asked Mom later, she just said something about an active imagination.

The dolls are even weirder. The Creep wouldn't let me touch them, she just held them up, and I couldn't see their faces or anything, but I could see enough to tell it's not a normal dollhouse family, with mom, dad, brother, and sister. Nothing's ever normal in our house anyway. No, this one's only got a dad, in a blue suit, a white-haired grandma, who I think has glasses, and a girl with dark hair. It looked like one of her legs was funny, like from a different doll or something. Maybe old Fowler tried to fix it after it lost a leg.

Kind of strange, their daughter having polio and all, with a lame doll, too.

Lina

September 17:

It's great, not having to kick the Creep out of my room. She doesn't even listen in on my phone calls anymore.

Actually, I'm kind of worried about her. All she ever does when she comes home from school is play with that stupid house. She keeps her curtains shut all the time, too. Mom sort of just stays away from Charlie's room now. I mean, I see her looking at Charlie's door like she wants to knock or go in or something, but she doesn't, she just hurries by.

The lawyer's red car is still parked out front. Maybe he's letting the gardener use it, though I don't see the gardener around much. Once I did, though, and he scared me. He was at the roses, and I thought it was old Fowler himself. What a nightmare that would be.

Lina

September 20:

Great news! Mom's quitting her job! She was so happy she was dancing around the kitchen, like she used to. She got another letter today from some lawyers, I guess the ones that guy in the blue suit works with. It turned out the Fowlers didn't have any relatives and left us money to live on. They left us the house, too, the one we're living in, though they're still trying to sell the little house next door.

Imagine, those awful people being so generous. Maybe now Mom'll see what's going on with Charlie and get her some help.

Lina

September 22:

Mom actually let Charlie stay home from school today. It's not like she's sick; she just doesn't want to go outside anymore. I guess Mom figured Charlie needs rest. I don't think so.

I went to check on Charlie when I got home. I mean, I'm her big sister, and if Mom doesn't do it, I guess I've got to. She keeps her room all dark now. I had to open the curtains, and she just sat on the floor in front of the dollhouse, blinking at me. I could've sworn her hair was darker.

I asked her about it. She just shrugged and stared, and I felt my skin go all prickly. Then she whined, "Shut the curtain, Lina," in her normal Creep way, so I felt better, but I ran to tell Mom anyway about the hair. I mean, maybe it's some kind of terrible disease. Maybe she got polio from the dollhouse.

Mom said it can't be, and it's probably just because she's inside so much. But I don't think hair changes color that fast. I checked the bathroom to see if she got into Mom's hair dyes, but there they were, neat and packaged like always. Mom just buys them, she never uses them. No one can see any gray in her hair anyway, except her.

Well, if Mom doesn't get that something's going on with Charlie, I guess it's up to me to figure it out. Maybe I'll play with her tomorrow, with the dollhouse, and see what happens.

Lina

September 23:

This is too much. Late last night I saw Charlie going down the hall, to the bathroom.

She was limping.

Lina

September 24:

I finally got Mom to look in on Charlie, but it was awful. It started when I knocked on her door this morning; she always keeps it closed now. She opened it a crack. She looked terrible, her hair all stringy and even darker and big circles around her eyes.

I asked if she'd play with me. She just looked at me like I was crazy. I said, "It isn't fair, you got the dollhouse, and all I want is to play with you for a while, no big deal. You know Mom always wants us to share."

Then Charlie goes, "It's not for sharing," in this weird, hollowlike voice.

I screamed for Mom. I couldn't help it. All of a sudden my little sister turned into this dark-haired, blank-eyed stranger and I don't know what's going on and I just needed Mom to come upstairs and fix it. She came running, two steps at a time.

I said, "Look," and pointed at Charlie standing there, bug-eyed. I told her about the limp.

At first Mom didn't go near Charlie. She just said, "It's time you let me in there, young lady,'' but I'd never heard her voice so shaky, not even when she fought with Daddy.

Charlie started whining and blaming it all on me, which made me feel better, since that's what she always does, but Mom didn't seem to feel better. She took a deep breath and stomped up, grabbed Charlie's wrist, pushed into her room and shut the door behind them.

I went to my room and listened through the wall. At first all I could hear was Mom shouting things like ''Answer me!'' and ''Stop staring!'' It was scary. Mom never shouts at us. Then they talked real low, and after a while I heard funny voices, like they were playing with the dollhouse together. I guess Mom and I had the same idea.

Mom came into my room later and said not to worry, it's just a stage Charlie's going through because of the Fowlers dying. She said Charlie's making up games about the dolls being the old Fowlers and she's the daughter. I reminded Mom that I'm the one that's supposed to look like their kid, and she said Charlie's jealous of all the attention the Fowlers paid me. I don't see why she'd be jealous of attention from those nasty old folks, the way everyone else always pets and coos over her, but I didn't want to start a fight.

Still, I had to ask about Charlie's hair, it didn't make sense, how it keeps getting darker. Mom said she probably got into the hair dye after all and threw the bottle in the outside garbage when she finished. Mom thinks maybe she's trying to look like the Fowlers' kid.

Then Mom said I should try to be more understanding, and we hugged. Maybe it was all that talk about hair, but when we hugged it was the first time I saw gray in Mom's. Maybe she really has been using those dyes.

Lina

September 28:

I haven't seen Charlie for days. Mom just brings her meals on trays and tells me to stay away from her room. Yesterday I saw a pair of glasses on one of the trays. Maybe Charlie's eyes are going bad because of how she keeps the room so dark now. I hope it isn't something like diabetes, that can make you blind.

At least Mom's spending lots of time playing dollhouse with her now. I feel better, with Mom helping her. I just wish Mom didn't look so tired and worried.

Lina

September 30:

It was all a fake! Things aren't getting better. I'd get out of here if I had anyplace to go, but it's not like I live in a normal family with aunts or grandparents or anything. Mom's all I've got. Or had.

It's the glasses. Tonight, at dinner, she had

them on, these big, thick, bottle-lens glasses, like the Fowlers used to wear. I asked where she got them. She just took them off and said she didn't remember, and why was I bothering about those old things anyway.

The thing is, Mom never wore glasses before.

Lina

October 2:

I can't stand it anymore. I tried to sneak out last night. I figured I'd go to a friend's or the police or anywhere, but Mom was on the phone and heard me. She asked where I was going. I couldn't say anything. She just took my bag back up to my room and told me to go to bed. She didn't even kiss me good night.

I thought about trying to sneak out again later, but her voice sounded so creaky, like she was really old. I got all worried about her. What if she's catching whatever Charlie has? Somebody has to stay and take care of them.

So, for a minute there, I was even glad when she said she'd been on the phone with Uncle Jake and he was coming tomorrow to help out around the house. The problem is, why does Mom need help now that she doesn't go to work anymore?

The bigger problem is, I don't have any Uncle Jake.

Lina

October 3:

This is my last entry. I guess I'll make up

some diary or something to turn in to English, but I can't ever turn this in. Mr. Cayou'll think I'm crazy and tell *them* all about it. Besides, if I can put this journal in the right place, maybe there's hope. Maybe somebody who understands all about this stuff will find it, maybe in another dimension or something. Just maybe.

I snuck into Charlie's room late last night, after Mom started snoring. Mom didn't used to snore.

I almost screamed when I saw that Charlie was gone and there was this thing on her bed. I don't know what else to call it. I didn't want to get close to it, but I had to get a better look, so, even though I was shaking all over and everything, I went to the bed, real slow. I guess I was afraid it would jump up and grab me all of a sudden, like in a monster movie, but it just lay there, not moving or breathing or anything. I couldn't make myself touch it. It looked wooden, like a life-size doll with dark hair. I've never seen a dead person, but I don't think it looked like one. It had color, like its face was painted. And it had this weird leg, like it belonged to something else, like the dollhouse daughter had.

I got real scared about Charlie, and then I *had* to look at the dollhouse. I didn't want to. Just thinking about it made me quivery and sick to my stomach. But I had to. I turned. Then it was all I could see, this big, dark house with stairs and windows just like ours, but not real, just sitting there, waiting, in Charlie's little room. It was really dark, there wasn't any moon outside. I had to get up close to see, since I didn't want to turn on any lights and wake up that thing on the bed or whatever.

I knelt by it. Charlie had put the dad in the attic room that Daddy had used for an office. It was looking out the window, its back to me. The daughter and grandma were lying face-down in what could have been Charlie's room.

I picked up the dad doll first. It felt so little and delicate, I was surprised Charlie could play with it so much without breaking it. I stroked its back. Its suit was really nice, with heavy, blue material. Old Mrs. Fowler probably sewed the clothes, I thought. Then I turned the doll over and nearly threw up. My skin prickled, like when I talked to Charlie before. I was shaking. My stomach got real tight. Everything went red. I nearly dropped the doll.

It had the face of the Fowlers' lawyer.

The thing on the bed behind me still didn't move. Mom was still snoring next door. It was still dark in the room. Everything was as it had been, but everything was different.

I started to reach for the daughter doll, but I couldn't touch it. Even with it lying down, I could see it wasn't the same as before. It didn't have a weird leg. It was blond and curly-haired, like Charlie used to be. And the grandma doll next to it didn't have white hair anymore, either. Now her hair was black. Like Mom's.

I guess that's when I screamed, real loud, I couldn't stop, I just kept screaming, even after the door flew open and old Mr. and Mrs. Fowler started shaking me and scolding me to stop, I'd wake the neighborhood. Mrs. Fowler was wearing Mom's nightgown.

"What've you done? What've you done?" I couldn't say anything else. I just kept saying "What've you done?" over and over and over.

Mr. Fowler sniveled. "Algebra," he said.

Then they said a whole lot of words, but I was shivering and crying so hard I could barely hear. I couldn't look at them, only at the dollhouse. It seemed so little and breakable now.

Mrs. Fowler said something about Jake being brilliant and how he made the doll that was on Charlie's bed for one of his first experiments to try to save their daughter.

Then Mr. Fowler started explaining. I couldn't understand all he said, but I'll write down what I remember, because maybe someday, if somebody ever finds this, they'll need to know that stuff to help me.

He said his first experiment didn't work because their daughter died too soon to make the "exchange" with the doll he built, the thing lying on Charlie's bed. He said it was all "thermodynamics" and "dimensionality." Energy, or heat, can never be destroyed, he said, but it isn't just transformed like everybody thinks. It travels, it goes places we don't know about yet. He said he can predict where it's going with fractals, and then he can exchange it, I think he said "at its point of turning with something of a similar kind in the destinational dimension." He said that's how to change dimensions. Or realities.

I couldn't stop shaking, I couldn't catch my breath, and my teeth were chattering, but the words just came out anyway, in hiccups: "I—thought—you—were—dead—"

Mr. Fowler started snickering and wiping his nose. Mrs. Fowler said how he'd learned to make these new dolls, but they're more like life-size models of real people. He got so good at it, the ones he made of them for their own "exchange" even fooled the paramedics. And then she said how kind it was of that "nice lawyer" to fix it so there weren't any autopsies, like they'd said in their wills. She was petting the doll in the blue suit as she talked.

It made me sick. I couldn't watch her, I couldn't move, I couldn't look at the dolls or even at the dollhouse. All I could do was stare at the tiny rosebushes set so neatly around it.

Then Mrs. Fowler talked about me going to school like always and staying in my house and then I could hear her words real clear like they were the only sound in the whole world.

"You're our daughter now, Nina. You'll live

with your dear Aunt Angela and Uncle Jake, until your mother and sister return from their travels. If they do."

That's when I looked at her. She grinned. I thought for sure she was going to eat me. She said if I was good and did everything they said, they'd take good care of the dollhouse and its dolls.

Then Mr. Fowler said, "Welcome to the other dimension, Nina."

So now you know. Since you're reading this, it means you found the pages I'm tearing out to hide behind the wallpaper, where the Fowlers won't find them. Maybe you understand. Maybe you know all about fractals and thermodynamics. Maybe you can help me. In the meantime, I'm desperately studying algebra.

What a nightmare.

Nina

Poems and nightmares speak to us in images.
Here is a poem that captures those images,
captures the essence of a nightmare.

BAD DREAM

Joan Aiken

This boy
got caught in his own dream
it was a dream about moss
hanging from branches
and about water
growing upwards like a tree
it was a dream about cats
like black holes in the wall
about birds in reverse
about time like a knife blade
bending sideways
it was a bad dream to get caught in
he began to scream

in this dream things were all bright and black
leaves were metal bars
a tortoiseshell moon

Bad Dream

snapped its comb-teeth
a dragon lay waiting
under an enormous leaf
in this dream trouble was underfoot
hidden and rustling
in this dream the sun was low
sidelong and unkind
pointing a sly finger
across his mind
it was a bad dream to be caught in
he struggled to turn back

in this dream a fluttering roar overhead
sucked off his fingernails
stairs led neither up nor down
but sideways into space
in this dream motion turned inward
like a purse
and some things flickered
that should have kept still
and things that ought to move
did not
which was worse
and nothing had much of a shape
and his head was a lid
it was a bad dream to be caught in.

Did he ever escape?
I never heard that he did.

There's one simple way to avoid nightmares: Don't sleep. The question is, how long can you stay awake?

THE GRAVEKEEPER

Patrick Bone

In a dark corner of the parlor, the boy huddled. Everywhere he looked he saw dolls. Miniature dolls in glass cabinets; fat, smiling baby dolls; and replicas of older children. They were made from plastic, ceramic, cloth, wood, and some materials he didn't recognize. The smallest dolls he ignored. But the life-size mannequins—there were many—sent shivers down his spine.

Facing him, a Victorian boy in brown corduroy knickers and a forest green jacket posed on a half-size blue velvet settee. His reddish hair was like the boy's own, and the brown eyes, though unblinking, followed him wherever he moved. The boy shuddered and whispered, "You almost might have been alive once." Then he touched his own auburn hair and blinked his brown eyes to make sure they still moved.

He thought of Mother. So unreal when he last saw her. They had dressed her in a white satin gown and placed the body gently in the coffin. He could still see her face. Ashen under the makeup, almost like . . . a mannequin's. Now, in this strange place, he found himself wondering, could she be a doll somewhere?

A tear rolled down his cheek. He felt embarrassed and looked at the red-haired doll across from him. Its expression remained the same. But those eyes. So alive! *Like he's watching me.* The boy worried he might be losing his mind.

The social worker had brought him to the house where she said his grandfather lived. She called him "the Dollmaker."

"He's your only living relative, Gabriel, dear," she had explained as she led him past the gate that hung on one rusted hinge, up the weed-covered footpath toward the house. She sighed, a prissy, oh-well sigh, and said, "He's a bit eccentric, you know. Says he doesn't want you. Something about the Gravekeeper." She paused at the top of the sagging front gallery. "Imagine that, the Gravekeeper."

Gabriel could still hear the hollow sound as she knocked. He could still smell the mint on her breath when she bent over so her face looked straight into his. "Don't listen to what he tells you. There is no Gravekeeper, young man, no Bogeyman who kidnaps and eats children."

He tried to keep from shuddering.

She laughed. "A children's story. He tells children's stories. Nobody believes him."

The door creaked open and an old man emerged from the shadow of the darkened foyer. Unsmiling, ancient, deformed from arthritis. Two knotty canes supported his twisted body. A maroon robe clung to him like the pall on a corpse.

It was their first meeting. Funny, Gabriel mused, how Mother always avoided speaking of him, never explained why they lived so far away and never visited.

The boy stared at the old face, studied the wrinkles twisted around the eyes and mouth like dried leather. He was sure he saw pain there. The old man put a gnarled hand to his bald head and rubbed the crooked fingers across his scalp. When he spoke, his words were measured. "He must not stay. It is the time . . . of the Gravekeeper."

The social worker handed him the papers and said, "It is the law. You have no choice until we find suitable foster parents."

The old man pointed a gnarled finger in the direction of the boy's room.

It took Gabriel a full day to become hungry. He found the kitchen and remnants of food in the larder. He understood he was on his own. The old man stayed in his own room and made no effort to speak with him. On the second day, when Gabriel dared to explore outside, he discovered the house sat alone in a narrow wooded valley where only filtered sunlight penetrated the trees. Wind and rain had turned the wooden one-story house a ghostly gray.

Inside, black drapes, drawn against the cold, kept the rooms dark and allowed beads of moisture to run races down the papered walls. At night, blue winds howled like voices of the dead. The boy was sure it was the dead because only yards behind the house, in a stand of twisted elms, lay an abandoned graveyard. He thought to investigate it, but whenever he got close, the smell of something putrid pushed him away.

But it was not the foul smell, nor the winds, nor even the graveyard that unsettled the boy. It was the dolls. He told himself he was too old for such fantasy. Still, he feared them.

The dolls occupied every room except his bedroom at the very back of the house near the cemetery. They were all sizes. Some looked real, others like regular dolls. Some innocent, a few funny, but not many. Others, the boy thought, looked evil. He tried not to believe an ugly thought that had invaded his imagination: *Do they come to life when I sleep?*

On the third night, as Gabriel lay in his bed,

he heard the pine plank flooring creak, followed by a tap, then another creak and a tap. Someone was in the hallway outside his room. The creaking and tapping stopped. He watched the knob turn and the door swing open. Gabriel made out the twisted shape of his grandfather in the dark doorway.

The man's voice was barely a whisper. "Come, boy. I have something to show you."

The Dollmaker's workshop lay hidden in the attic. Tools and doll parts occupied the workbench. Arms, legs, hair, and heads lay scattered across the floor and in corners like dismembered corpses, while other pieces dangled by strings from the rafters. The smell of mold and paints and glue made the boy feel faint. On either side, two small windows allowed the fumes to escape.

The old man stopped to catch his breath after the steep climb up the steps, then shuffled to an oak desk where he set a match to a lantern. Blue flame flickered. For the first time he looked Gabriel in the eye.

"Stand closer," he said. "There's something you must see."

The old man opened a drawer and retrieved a gray ledger book. "Each of my dolls has a story," he said. "I have recorded them in my ledgers. Their stories are true. You must believe that."

Gabriel shivered. He wanted to run, but his grandfather took his wrist and pulled him closer. The strength in the old man's hand surprised him. A scent of decay whiffed from the Dollmaker's mouth when he said, "You *must* hear this one story if you are to survive."

He opened the book and turned the pages with a rigid finger. Gabriel saw sketches of dolls and scribbled notes flash by in the candlelight. His grandfather stopped near the end of the ledger.

"There!" he said. "The Gravekeeper."

A crude, evil-looking face stared out at the boy like a nightmare. He jumped back.

The drawing depicted a dark person, dressed in a tattered overcoat, with a great brimmed hat half-covering his eyes. The creature hovered over a crib. In one hand he held a dirty burlap gunnysack; in the other, a sleeping child.

A muffled cry escaped Gabriel's mouth, and he tried to pull away, but the Dollmaker held him tighter. "It is the Gravekeeper," he said. "The stories are true, and tomorrow comes the Harvest Moon. You must prepare."

"I . . . but . . ." The words would not come.

The Dollmaker pulled him closer, so close their faces touched. "Don't run," he said. "When you hear the story, you will understand."

"Just after the Civil War, a young man was

retained to care for the graveyard here. He was a veteran, wounded so he dragged his leg from place to place. But he kept the graveyard free of weeds, planted the grass and flowers, and cultivated the tiny plot until some said it was the queen of cemeteries. He was paid poorly: pennies a month for supplies, which he always plowed back into the land. Then, when he was an old man, too old to find another job, too old even to keep the weeds from choking the flowers, something very sad happened."

Gabriel couldn't contain himself and asked, "What was that, Grandfather?"

When the boy called him "Grandfather," the Dollmaker smiled and continued. "The county fathers said to him, 'Your services are no longer needed.' "

Gabriel whispered, "He was fired."

"Yes, let go," Grandfather said, "and that's when something worse came to pass."

The boy's eyes grew wide.

The old man looked around the attic as if they might not be alone. Then he said, "The Gravekeeper begged them for money, a small pension so he would not starve. They laughed, scorned him from their presence. 'We are not responsible for your welfare,' one said. 'So far as I am concerned, you may eat dogs.' "

"Oh, no," Gabriel said.

"Oh, yes," the Dollmaker responded, "he had no choice. Half mad from hunger and hu-

miliation, the Gravekeeper ate whatever small animal—cat or dog—he could capture. Soon the animals were depleted or locked tight in their houses. Then it happened. One night, the night of the Harvest Moon, when winds raged and the Gravekeeper could no longer keep warm in his cemetery hiding place, the first child disappeared."

"The Gravekeeper?" Gabriel asked.

The Dollmaker shrugged. "Perhaps. It was never proved. But he was discovered, dragged from hiding, and tied by the neck to an elm tree in the graveyard. It was said he died slowly."

"But, Grandfa—"

"You want to know what that has to do with you?"

"You said the Gravekeeper died."

"Indeed! So it seemed. But the next year, on the Harvest Moon, another child disappeared. Then another, and another, for three days. The county fathers revisited the Gravekeeper's grave. The body was gone."

The boy felt a cold wind across the back of his neck. He turned slowly, but saw nothing in the dark corners of the attic.

"You must know the rest," his grandfather said. "Every year, after he died, children disappeared. During the three nights of the Harvest Moon, children in the valley disappeared. At first everyone denied the stories. Everyone, that is, except the parents who lost children. Eventually most moved away. No children remained. Then the legend died. Newcomers moved to the valley, strangers like your grandmother and me.

"At first we didn't believe the old ones. But I listened to their tales all the same, and the more I listened, the more I learned. It was said he came only during the Harvest Moon. It was said he could not be kept from entering a home, and there was no way to escape him once he selected his child victim. Except . . ."

"Except what, Grandfather?"

"Except that he could be bought off by parents who awaited his arrival with food, enough raw meat to last one year." The old man paused. "You've noticed it, boy, from the graveyard, the smell of rotting flesh."

The boy nodded. Then a question crossed his mind. "Did the Gravekeeper come for my mother?"

The Dollmaker smiled. "Every Harvest Moon, until your mother would no longer fit into the Gravekeeper's sack, I remained awake in her room and kept vigilance. There were years when he did not come. But then he did. I was terrified. He looked . . . like this."

The old man pointed to the sketch. "Only much larger, great hands hardened by years of work, his features I could not see for the wide-brimmed hat that fell like a shadow across his face. He did not speak, but simply held out the sack and shook his head. I filled it with raw meat. Then he left as he had come. Now you can understand why your mother never visited."

"Why, Grandfather?"

His grandfather sighed. "She thought me crazy. Your mother never saw the Gravekeeper because I protected her from him. No child wants to believe in monsters. Not real monsters, not monsters who eat children. She never saw the Gravekeeper, and she was ashamed of me because I told the old stories." He searched the boy's eyes. "Do *you* believe me, boy?"

"Yes, Grandfather."

"Then there is something else you must know to survive the next three nights."

The boy took a deep breath. "Please tell me."

His grandfather measured each word. "You must understand, I can no longer buy your safety. The larder is almost empty. There is no meat. And I cannot stay awake to protect you. But there is a way."

Gabriel said, "A way?"

"You must not sleep. For the next three nights, when the Gravekeeper wanders, you must not close your eyes, not even a moment. For he waits until a child sleeps to work his ghoulish spell."

So that's it, the boy thought. *I must face the monster and stare it down.*

"I can do that," he said. But in his heart, he wondered if he had the courage.

Gabriel sat in bed, the dim light of a coal-oil lantern illuminating the book in his lap. He looked about. Behind the headboard a draped window still allowed a chilling draft. When the wind blew, the window frames shook as if the house itself were afraid of what would soon happen.

Except for a pine chest, there was no furniture, only a closet to the right of the bed. Gabriel did not like the closet. *A wonderful place for a monster to hide,* he thought.

Past midnight he heard something outside the house. A sudden bolt of lightning crashed in the graveyard, and Gabriel felt his heart jump into his throat. For several minutes the wind howled fiercely. Then it died. At first the silence felt good. Then Gabriel heard the noise again. *Something far away,* he thought. The wind started. A rotten, pungent odor wafted through the windows.

He dropped his book to the floor. *I must look outside,* he thought. Carefully he reached over and blew out the lamp to keep from being seen. For a moment he listened in the dark. *There!* He heard it again. *Something in the graveyard. I'm sure of it.* Carefully he eased from the covers and turned toward the headboard. On his knees he pulled the drapes apart.

For minutes there was nothing. He felt sleepy and thought, *Maybe it's my imagination. Perhaps if I close my eyes just for a moment* . . . That's when he saw it. The moon was bright in the old cemetery, casting eerie shadows across the ground through twisted elm branches. *Maybe that's what it is,* he thought, *shadows from the trees.* Then he saw it again. This time, for sure. Something moved from tree to tree, something large and dark, something dragging an object like a gunnysack behind it. The boy blinked and it was gone.

He waited, his eyes wide in terror and curiosity. An hour. Two hours. Nothing. Then, off in the distance, a child's cry. Or the wind? He prayed, *Please let it be the wind.* But he was sure he had also heard the sound of something dragged across the ground.

"No," he whispered, "this is not happening. It's my imagination."

He closed the drapes and sat down.

When dawn broke, he was tired but still awake. "Now I can sleep," he said to himself. But he couldn't fall asleep. Nor could he admit for sure he had seen the Gravekeeper.

He feared leaving the house. Instead, he wandered among the dolls. They no longer seemed threatening, even the boy on the blue velvet settee. *After last night,* he thought, *nothing in this house can scare me.*

He was wrong. While he munched on a carrot at the kitchen table, he heard scratching noises. A slender door he had paid no attention to before stood ajar. He tiptoed across the room and was about to peek inside when the door flew open and the boy looked into the eyes of his grandfather.

"What is it?" the man said.

The boy started to answer, but the words died in his throat when he saw what stood behind his grandfather. A doll—at least he hoped so. A life-size doll, wearing a dark overcoat and a hat that covered the face like a shadow. The boy gasped and stumbled backward.

The Dollmaker shrugged. "I showed you the drawing, boy. Did you think I would not make the doll?"

The boy wanted to run, but he forced himself to speak. "Why, Grandfather?"

"Because I am the Dollmaker. Because there is no one left to warn the newcomers. No one else to tell the stories." The old man studied Gabriel's face. "I know what you're thinking. No one believes me. They think I'm crazy. You're wondering if they are right. You want to know why I never left?"

Gabriel nodded.

The old man's eyes seemed to turn cold. He squared his shoulders. "Perhaps because I am crazy. Perhaps because when your grandmother died and it was said I had become insane, I could no longer sell my dolls and there was no place else to go. Or perhaps someone had to stay to tell the stories of the children."

"The other dolls?" the boy said.

The grandfather nodded. "All have their stories, boy. I told you. Once I made dolls for patrons throughout the world. The Master, they called me. Now I make my dolls to remember the dead, and to frighten away those who would become the dead. I tell their stories as I understand them, not in words, but in the art of the Dollmaker."

Gabriel felt faint. He grasped for something to say. "The boy with red hair on the parlor sofa. What is his story?"

The Dollmaker sighed. "He was an innocent boy. He went to school. He had friends. And then he was eaten. Eaten by the Gravekeeper."

The boy ran. He did not want to hear any more, and he felt he could no longer believe his grandfather. Dead men do not come to life. There had to be another explanation, a logical one, one he feared more than the lies of the old man.

That night, though he doubted his grandfather's story, he could not let himself fall asleep. By the middle of the night, Gabriel had done all he could to stay awake. He splashed water on his face from a pitcher he had brought into the bedroom. He slapped himself, breathed deeply to keep his blood flowing. He tried reading, then threw aside the book as its pages drew him toward sleep. He paced the floor, no longer afraid of making noises. Finally, near four o'clock, he felt cold, went back to bed, and pulled the covers to his head. "Two more hours," he whispered, "two more hours till dawn."

Against his will, his eyes began to close. Then he smelled a sick odor and heard something outside his window. *Oh, no,* he thought, *he's closer now, much closer than last night.*

Gabriel turned in his bed, extinguished his lantern, and reached for the drapes. "I must see him," he whispered. "I must see if he looks like grandfather."

Slowly he opened the curtains, and for a moment all he could discern was darkness. Clouds hid the moon and with it the light that lit the cemetery. The boy edged his face closer to the window just as the clouds parted, and he thought he saw his own face in the pane. But when his eyes adjusted, he realized it wasn't his reflection at all.

What he saw made his blood run cold and his heart pound so he feared he would pass out. He tried to pull the drapes together, but his arms wouldn't move. His mind told him, *There is a face in the window, the face of a dark man, someone wearing a wide-brimmed hat that covers his features, someone evil who has selected his next victim. The Gravekeeper has arrived.*

Then, as quickly as he came, he was gone.

In a moment Gabriel heard scraping sounds. The way the old man would walk without his canes? He could imagine the Dollmaker's deformed legs dragging the ground, and the gunnysack . . . He didn't want to think about that, nor about what happened next.

He heard a child's voice. No doubt, this time. A child cried, "Please, let me go home!"

Next day Gabriel avoided the Dollmaker. But when darkness fell and winds howled, he found himself drawn to the old man. A fearful thought gripped him. *Has he worked a spell on me? How do I know the old man is really my grandfather anyway?*

But the boy had not slept in two days, and as the light faded, his eyelids fell closed more often. He knew he couldn't stay awake another night. So he swallowed his doubts and looked for the Dollmaker. He found Grandfather in the parlor where he sat peacefully in the company of his dolls.

Gabriel said, "I'm afraid, Grandfather."

The old man turned to him. "I know."

"May I stay in your room tonight?"

The Dollmaker shook his head. "I'm too old. As you have seen, I sleep often, even during the day. But that is not the reason you may not seek comfort with me tonight. If you stay with me, you will lose your fear and fall asleep.

Understand this, my grandchild, fear is not the enemy. It is your friend. It will keep your senses sharp tonight, and you will find a way. I can say no more. Except . . ."

"Except, Grandfather?"

"Except he will try harder tonight. You must be strong, resourceful. Use your wits, my boy! Remember, he cannot work his spell so long as he sees your eyes."

The monster was in the house.

The boy watched as the Gravekeeper pushed open the door to his room and dragged his leg across the bedroom floor until he stood at the foot of the bed.

Gabriel willed himself not to move. The Gravekeeper lifted his gunnysack, looked inside, and shook his head from side to side. There was no sound, only the damp graveyard smell that crawled across the floorboards like a deadly fog. And the Gravekeeper waited.

Two hours passed while the boy and Gravekeeper kept their silent vigil, the boy's eyes wide and afraid, the Gravekeeper's half-shielded by his hat. *Dawn will come soon,* Gabriel thought. Then a sudden coolness came to him, and he felt peaceful and unafraid. *I can do this forever,* he thought. *I can stay awake forever.* Only his eyes betrayed him.

They felt heavy, so heavy he had to hold them open with his hands. *Stay awake,* he told himself. But the calmness settled over him, and his hands dropped to his sides. In his mind, music played, and he saw himself running in the sunshine. But outside it was dark. There would be no sun for another hour.

That's when Gabriel's eyes closed, and he fell into a deep, dark sleep.

Faint rays of dawn crept into the bedroom from the corners of the drapes. The old doll-maker stood at the foot of the bed and shook his head. "Where is the boy?" he whispered to himself.

"Where are you, Gabriel?" he shouted hoarsely.

In the bed lay a Victorian boy—not real, but a doll—the same size as Gabriel himself, with red hair and brown eyes, the kind of eyes that never blink and that follow you wherever you go. The doll wore the boy's pajamas. That's when the Dollmaker looked over at the closet and saw it was ajar a fraction of an inch.

"Ah," he said. "A wonderful place for a boy to hide!"

He woke Gabriel, who slept sitting up on the closet floor, where he had watched the monster through the slit in the door.

The boy stretched and smiled.

"You were very resourceful," his grandfather said, "very resourceful, indeed."

"Stay calm" is good advice. But when your world is falling apart around you, it can be hard to keep your head.

GONE TO PIECES

Michael Stearns

My parents' divorce hit me pretty hard.

I was a real sap about it, stumbling around in a daze for weeks. I moped and I mumbled and I stared at my feet, and every now and then, used the pass at school to go to the restroom, where I would sit in one of the smelly stalls and feel sorry for myself. My grades dive-bombed, the customers on my paper route complained about how sloppy I'd become, my friends called me a downer and stopped coming over.

Everyone, that is, except for Scott.

Scott just said, "Jeeze, Roy, that bites," and started inviting me over to his house more often. He didn't mind if I was bummed out. He let me be depressed while we watched TV or sorted our baseball cards or just sat in his backyard watching his dog chase its tail.

Then one morning a few weeks before Christmas, Scott told me, "Yo, my parents are getting divorced, too." Just like that. I about fell out of my chair, but Scott just shrugged and spooned some raisin bran into his mouth.

We were eating breakfast. Every day after I threw my papers, I pedaled over to Scott's house and ate with him while his mom got ready for work. Then he and I biked to school.

Suddenly the past week made sense: I hadn't seen Scott's dad slouching around, and his mom was always on the sniffly verge of tears. Even the dog seemed kind of glum. But Scott acted like everything was the same as always.

"You must feel pretty lousy," I said.

He looked thoughtful for a second. "Nah. It's no big deal."

That's when his head fell off.

His neck split right in the middle and his head slid forward like a pile of books off a crooked shelf. Scott caught it just before it splashed into his cereal bowl. On either side of his neck were flat empty stretches of skin like rubbed-down Silly Putty.

"Scott," I said, "your head, um—"

He stared down into his cereal and said, "No kidding, Holmes. Good thing I didn't already comb my hair, huh?"

"Wow," I whispered. "I'll get your mom."

"No," he said, and shifted his head around

in his hands so he could look at me. "Have you seen her lately? She can't do anything."

"What about a doctor?"

"I don't think this is that kind of problem, Roy."

"So what do we do?"

"What do you think we do? We reattach the stupid thing."

In the dank chill of Scott's garage I duct-taped a sawn-off broomstick to his back. Then, balancing his head on the smooth pink stump of his neck, I wrapped a sweatband of tape around his forehead and the broomstick.

"Hey," he said. "This works all right." The broomstick started to shift, and he grabbed at his head. "Better tape it at the neck, too."

I did that, then pulled him in front of the mirror his dad had hung in one corner of the garage. Scott turned in profile, peered at his reflection, then turned back. "Dorky, but not bad."

I checked my watch. "We're going to be late for school."

Scott slumped—or tried to; he winced against the broomstick. "Maybe I should just hang here."

"No way," I said, and thought desperately for a moment. "Let's go to Larry's. He'll know what to do."

"Good idea," Scott said. "If anyone knows, I guess it would be Larry."

"Better bring the tape," I said, tossing it into the corner of the huge basket I carried my papers in.

Scott awkwardly climbed onto his bike, stabbed at the garage-door opener, and we set off.

Winter hadn't hit yet but was hanging about, and the sky stayed socked in gloom until almost seven-thirty each morning. The cold was depressing, and I wished it would snow already and quit all this playing around. The wind knew what was coming, though, and coursed down the road and into your jacket and socks and everything. When you rode in that wind, you struggled just to keep control of your bike.

We were numb by the time we turned off Scott's street.

"Whoa," Scott said. "This is going to be tough."

I looked back and saw him sitting straight up in his saddle. No one sits up straight in that kind of wind if they can help it, but Scott couldn't crouch down because of the broomstick. He was jerking his handlebars back and forth, shivering and wobbling all over the place.

"You going to make it to Larry's?" I asked.

He didn't answer.

Larry lived past the school, on the edge of the cemetery in a run-down cottage that he got rent-free for digging graves and taking care of the grounds. He mowed the plots and cleaned up the graffiti kids left on tombstones. But Larry's real art was knife-throwing. He'd worked in circuses and casinos and on television since before we were born. But for some reason he hadn't performed in years.

There was no real reason to think Larry could help Scott, no reason at all. But Larry was the closest thing we knew to a wise man. We usually just swapped baseball cards with him, but he knew other things. He knew things our parents didn't care about or had forgotten long ago. He was almost forty, but he knew how to juggle and do cartwheels, and he ate Froot Loops and drank Dr Pepper and read comic books. He was always the guy to find that rare baseball card or the quarter you lost at the movies, the guy whose stones skipped the most times, the guy who caught the biggest fish but threw them back because he didn't feel like eating fish anyway.

If anyone would be able to fix Scott, I knew, it would be Larry.

When we reached the bottom of the big hill before the school, Scott called to me.

"What's up?" I asked, coasting back to where he leaned on his bike in the middle of the road.

He gestured up the hill and said, "Can you go get my leg?"

I looked at him again, and suddenly I saw that his left leg was missing. One pantleg was flapping in the wind, empty.

"Better hurry up," he said, pointing, "before some car comes by and flattens it."

So I pumped back up the hill, crossing back and forth to get to the top, cursing with every breath. I was worried about Scott's leg. I was worried about *Scott.* It made my chest hurt to think about. I felt as bad as I had since my parents told me about their divorce. But I tried to keep my chin up. Larry would fix everything.

The leg was okay when I got to it, though awfully pale and phony-looking. Scott's sneaker and sock were still there, but the leg was cold to the touch, like a dead piece of meat you take out of the freezer. I shuddered, picked it up, and threw it into my basket with the tape. Then I turned around and rocketed back down the hill.

When I got to Scott, he had his right arm hanging in the crook of his left. I think he was trying to stuff it into his jacket. "This is getting worse," he said. He laughed weakly.

I took Scott's arm from him and set it in my basket on top of his leg. There was a squeak behind me, and I turned to find him on the ground, his other leg and arm lumpy in his clothes. "Wow," he said.

"Why don't we just lock your bike up here," I said, "and I'll carry you in my basket." I didn't wait for Scott's okay. He obviously couldn't make it on his own.

I threw his limbs into the basket, then hugged up his torso and set it on top of everything else, taking care to pull off the broomstick and tape. I wedged his head in one corner of the basket so that he could look at me as I pedaled. "Better?" I asked.

"Sure," he said. "I'm fine."

I left his bike by the side of the road and pedaled hard, talking to Scott the entire time, trying to convince him everything was going to be okay.

But I couldn't even convince myself.

I got quiet when we passed our school. Schools can do that to you sometimes. The sky was still smeared with darkness, but the building was squat and bright with light and looked warm and cozy. All around us, buses and cars were pulling in, and kids were streaming across the road. I had to dodge a few students as I zoomed past.

"I hope no one spots us going the wrong way," I said. "You doing okay?"

"I'm great," Scott said. He flinched. "Wow. I think my hands just fell off."

"Just hold yourself together a while longer," I said. "We'll be there soon."

I pulled right up onto Larry's front porch and rapped hard on the door. Larry sleeps pretty heavily; after his weekend boozing, it can be almost impossible to get him up. "Come on, Larry!" I shouted. "This is an emergency!"

The door swung open. Larry had on jeans and a T-shirt under the smelly robe he always wore at home. "Where's the fire, old boy?" he asked, smiling limply.

"It's Scott," I said. "Can we come inside?"

He looked around and sighed heavily. "Sure, kid, but the bike stays outside."

"Then you need to give me a hand with Scott."

He looked at the bike again, this time staring straight at the basket. His smile flattened out. "Oh, man. You guys are way too young for this kind of thing." He looked at the bruised sky and cinched his robe tight. "Better wheel him in."

Though the cottage was small, Larry's junk made it feel even smaller. I loved the clutter. An enormous wheel leaned against one wall; Larry used to strap his assistant to the wheel and spin it, then throw knives at it from thirty paces. And there were other neat things: mannequins and trophies, a collection of metal lunch boxes, a plastic skeleton in a coffin.

And on nearly every wall, there were photographs of Larry and the Woman. She was pretty in the way that some people in old photos are. Movie-star pretty. She had this long white neck and a wide smile of a mouth and dark hair that was always just a strand or two short of fashion-model perfect. You just knew that this woman was never anyone's mother or sister or wife; she existed just to hang on Larry's arm in photos. Once, while I was sorting baseball cards for him, I'd stopped to stare at a photo of her. It was nothing special—she was putting something into the trunk of a car—but it was clear she could barely stand up from laughing so hard.

"Stop staring," Larry had told me, "and get to work. You've got another three boxes to sort before I hand over Roberto Clemente."

I never asked about the Woman. Larry didn't allow it.

But I stared at her image now, while in the sticky warmth of the living room Larry checked Scott over. "Can you feel this?" he asked, pinching the skin on Scott's left elbow.

"Feel what?" Scott asked. His eyes were glassy and rolling in their sockets.

"Darn. This is far along." Larry sat back on his haunches and scratched at his beard.

"It happened real fast," I said.

"I bet it started here," Larry said, and thumped hard on Scott's chest.

"Yeah," Scott said. "Like heartburn. I drank

all this Pepto, but the ache wouldn't go away until . . ." Across the room, his shoulders twitched. "But I'm fine now."

Larry laughed. "Sure you're fine, but you look like the, the . . ." He nodded thoughtfully, then sat down backward on his piano bench. He'd never owned a piano. "Like the Ghost of Christmas Parts, Scott." Larry erupted into laughter. He laughed so hard at his joke that he fell off the bench.

Scott laughed, too. "That's terrible."

"This is no time for jokes, Larry," I said.

"On the contrary," Larry said, but stopped there. He laid a finger against Scott's neck—feeling for a pulse, I guess. "So what's gone bad in your life, Scott?"

"Nothing," Scott said. "Everything's cool."

"His parents are divorcing," I said.

Scott scowled. "That's not bothering me."

"Sure," Larry said. "You're a big guy, right? Too big a guy to feel bad about something as unimportant as your parents calling it quits."

"They do what they have to do. I'll get by," Scott said. Across the room, his right foot split off from his leg and dropped to the floor with a thump.

"So you don't feel sad at all?" While Larry talked, he rummaged through one of his piles of clothes until he produced a wrinkled trench coat, then switched it for the bathrobe.

"I'm cool," Scott said.

"Uh huh." Larry turned to me. "Roy, can you fit a pick and a shovel in that basket of yours, with . . . ?" He gestured toward Scott.

"I guess so. Why?"

"He's dying. It happens by degrees, you know? First you die inside. You stop caring. Then—*pppbbbttt.*" He snapped his fingers.

Scott said, "I'm not *dead* inside."

"But you don't care about your parents divorcing?"

"Well, I'm not going to get upset about it, I mean—" Scott's other foot fell.

"You see what I mean?"

"So what do we do?" I asked.

Larry smiled and winked at me. "The same thing we do with all the dead. We bury him."

"No way," I said. "We can't!" Everything *wasn't* going to be okay, I realized.

"Scott," Larry asked him, "how do you feel about us putting you six feet under? Does that bother you at all?"

If Scott could have shrugged, he would have. Instead, he just acted like he'd been acting all morning. "I'm down with that," he said. There were a couple of muffled bumps in the corner of the room.

"There go your knees," Larry commented.

Graveyards are scary to a lot of people, but—maybe because of Larry or maybe because back when my parents were together they regularly took me to visit my grandparents' graves—I've never had any trouble with tombstones and great lawns of the dead and all that. Sometimes when we'd go to Larry's to trade cards, he'd be out finishing up a grave, and we'd bike out into the green to find him standing down in the earth, his shovel working to even out the sides and bottom and make the hole look tidy. "It's just a hole," he said once when my friend Mike Romaneck goggled his eyes. "If there's anything frightening in here, you put it here yourself."

We rode out now past the older plots where gravestones and monuments still stood, all thorny with gargoyles and angels, to the more recent sites where plain plaques sat flat in the lawn.

"Won't you need the backhoe?" I asked, but Larry threw me a look that clearly meant *shut your mouth*. So I shut it.

"Where would you like to be buried?" Larry asked Scott.

Scott just blinked and said, "What do I care?"

"What do you mean, you don't care?" I blurted. "He's talking about *burying* you, you dip—aren't you paying attention?"

"What's it matter to me?" he asked, then fell silent.

We found an empty spot near a clutch of pine trees at the cemetery's edge. Larry toed down his kickstand and swung off his bike, then stripped off his jacket and threw it to the ground. He reached in my basket and raised Scott's head up to his face. "Alas, poor Scott . . . Where should I put you?" Scott didn't answer. "So that's how it's going to be, eh? Guess I'll just prop you where you can watch." He balanced Scott's head atop the soft pile of his jacket.

I just sat there on my bike. If I didn't get off, maybe Larry would stop this.

Larry looked at me and said, "Close your mouth, Roy. And get to work." I watched dumbly as he picked up the rest of Scott's body—his arms and legs, the blocky bulk of his torso, the handful of fingers and toes. He put everything down beside Scott's head, where Scott would be sure to see it. A single tear made a shiny path down Scott's cheek.

"You're hurting, aren't you?" Larry set the pick on the ground, laid the shovel next to it.

A muscle bulged in Scott's jaw as he clenched his teeth. "No," he said. His nose slid to the ground with a wet plop.

Larry squinted at him and nodded once, curtly. "Uh huh. You know the Pinnochio story, don't you?" Scott didn't answer. "Every time he lied, his nose got longer, right? It's similar when you're hurting. You can close it off, say you're not in pain, but you're going to fall apart sooner or later, in one way or another. You know what I mean?"

"But I'm *not* hurting," Scott insisted.

"Right," Larry said. He hefted up the pick and swung it into the ground with practiced ease. Clods of earth puckered up around the blade and came loose. He pulled them away and swung again.

Scott and I watched quietly. The wind sighed around us, as cold as the world can seem.

And I shivered. I shivered long and hard, shivered with the image of Scott lying jumbled in a fresh grave, dirt piled on his face. Shivered with the thought of the breakup of my family and the sadness back home. Shivered because, with Scott gone, I was truly alone. I felt sorry for Scott, but worse than that, I felt sorry for myself—and ashamed of my self-pity, and that only made everything worse. My chest heaved and I began to cry. Not like a dam breaking—nothing that wet and messy—just a steady trickle down the sides of my face, a trickle that grew chill in the wind.

"Roy, get off your butt and help me dig," Larry said.

I got off my bike and grabbed a shovel. The first bite of the blade in the ground was hard, but after that it was easy. I was getting mad, still crying and furious because of it—sobbing like an idiot and turning over shovelful after shovelful of dirt. I couldn't really see what I was doing through my tears, but after a moment it didn't matter. *If Scott wants to be bur-*

ied, I thought, *that's cool. If he doesn't care, that's his problem.* I'd been depressed before, and thanks to Scott I'd gotten over it. But I wouldn't go through that again. *To heck with you,* I thought at Scott. And the pain went away.

Just then, my left arm slid off and thumped to the ground. I blinked back my tears and looked at it. There was no pain. I felt nothing at all. When I flexed my fingers, the fingers on the hand wriggled. *No big deal,* I thought. Then my right arm came apart at the elbow. I sat down just as my left knee gave out, then felt my head tumbling forward into my lap. I blinked at an upside-down blur of trees and sky.

"Uh, Larry?"

I heard his digging pause, then the clang of his shovel dropping. "Oh no! Not you, too!"

I shrugged. "It happens."

Larry laughed, but he sounded nervous. "Yes, indeed." I felt his dirty fingers in my hair, and my head was turned and placed in my lap facing forward.

Scott didn't laugh, though his face was animated for the first time all day, his eyebrows down and his teeth clenched. Another tear rolled down his face. "What's the matter with you, Roy? Pull yourself together!"

"Oh, that's rich," Larry said. "Humpty-Dumpty all gone to pieces but telling someone else to keep himself together. Oh ho."

Scott's face wrinkled up with rage. "Shut up! Shut up! What do you know about anything? You don't know what I'm going through, you don't know what it's like to have everything fall apart! You don't know jack—"

"Sure I do," Larry said quietly. He raised his right arm and pulled back his cuff. Zig-zagging around his wrist was a scribble of heavy black thread. Stitches. He'd once come apart, too.

"I've been there. Have fallen down so hard that I didn't care whether or not I got up again. After Emma passed away . . . A friend put me back together, and after that I just held myself together however I could." He regarded his wrist. "I left this bit of thread to remind me."

Scott was silent, but he was really crying now, worrying his lip with his teeth. "It's too late. Look at me. I couldn't get myself back together even if I wanted to."

"Nonsense," Larry said, and squatted down in front of us. "All you have to do is want to. But you have to *really* want to. If you don't truly care . . ."

"But it hurts, Larry," Scott said, and then he wailed. I joined him. We sounded like a couple of big babies.

Larry nodded. "I know it hurts. I know. But that pain, that's how you know you're alive."

He taped us both back up, Larry did, giving us two-inch-thick cuffs around our wrists and ankles, swaddling our joints in so much gray tape that we were rigid as the dead afterward. He muttered the whole time about how messy this business was, how Elmer's Glue was really the way to go, but tape would have to work until we got a hold of ourselves. "We'll put your fingers on when we get back to my place," he said. "I've got some glue there."

"No thread?" Scott asked.

"Not unless you want to be the Ghost of Christmas Suture!" Larry howled.

We groaned.

Then I thought about having to peel the tape *off.* "It's going to kill," I told Scott. "Imagine having your whole body covered in Band-Aids."

"But what good is this, Larry?" Scott asked. "We're only taped up."

"Sure, for now you're just taped. But soon you'll feel things go back to normal. You'll feel a click somewhere down deep, like your heart hiccuping or your soul snapping back or . . . something. And you'll know. Trust me on this."

I did. And as we walked our bikes stiff-limbed toward Larry's place, it began to snow.

Scott laughed and said we could finally go sledding, and I laughed in agreement, and then I realized something was happening. My whole body was tingling, like I'd slept on it wrong. It hurt a bit. "Yikes!" I said. "I'm all pins and needles."

"That just means you're healing," Larry said. "It'll last a few weeks."

"A few *weeks?*" Scott and I asked at the same time.

"Hey," Larry laughed, "I never said this was going to be easy."

Sheesh.

Some creatures will eat anything. . . .

IT CAME FROM THE CLOSET

Andrew Fry

One night before he went to bed,
A small young boy named Jonny said,
"There's something in my closet, Dad.
It's big and hairy and really mad.
It ate the dog, it ate my toys,
It frightened all the other boys.
It ate my socks, it ate my coat,
It even ate a sticky note.
It ate my hat, it ate my shoes,
It ate the plastic cow that moos.
It ate my shirt, it ate my pants,
It ate my book called *How to Dance.*
And then it ate my underwear,
And that explains why I am bare!"

I live in the snowiest city in the United States. So this story has special meaning for me.

SNOW

Al Sarrantonio

On the day before Christmas, a few rogue snowflakes fell. They drifted like unsure intruders; dropped, reluctant parachutists, from a sky still clear and blue-cold with Autumn. They fell on Eva's nose and melted, fell onto Charles' outstretched tongue and were warmed into water.

"I wish it would snow forever!" Eva said.

"And ever!" Charles said.

"We'd build forts and go sledding!"

"Have snowball fights and dig tunnels!"

"Forever!" Eva said.

"And ever!" said Charles.

"We'd never have to go to school again!"

"Hurrah!"

And, in other places, other Charleses and other Evas said the same things.

The skies darkened.

It began to snow.

* * *

It snowed on Christmas—all twelve days of it. It snowed, inch upon inch of white, falling in flat layers from an always-gray sky.

Eva and Charles sledded, drank hot chocolate, and cheered. They had snowball fights, and built forts.

And still it snowed.

It snowed for twenty days, then twenty days more. Each day it snowed. Drifts sat on snow drifts. There were layers of snow, geologic demarcations, that traced the storm's history.

School was canceled again and again.

Eva and Charles cheered, played Monopoly inside as snow layers climbed up the sliding glass door of the family room, topped Mother's bushes, made their tiny twig fingers wave goodbye as they went under.

It snowed.

And snowed.

And . . .

Snowed.

"It's never going to stop," Mother said, staring out at the snow with her haggard face, a cold cup of tea nestled forgotten in her hands. "It's going to snow forever."

"And ever!" Charles laughed, and then he and Eva went out to build another snow fort as Father, in the driveway, cursed his snowblower, which coughed and then died.

It snowed.

And snowed.

And snowed some more.

There was no school, and then there was no mail. There were no packages. The stores, the malls, the 7-Elevens, winked out one by one. People drew into their homes like ticks, battling their walks and driveways before finally giving up. Snowplows roared, then died like dinosaurs at the end of their reign. They plowed sideways into curbs and then sputtered out, their drivers hopping out as if afraid, tramping hurriedly home through the disappearing streets.

It snowed.

And snowed.

Eva and Charles played, built walls of snow that were eaten, threw snowballs that were swallowed. Soon they could almost reach the house's gutters with their mittens. They ran huffing in to drink the last of the hot chocolate, topped by the last of the marshmallows.

It continued to snow.

And snow.

And snow.

And then:

"I'm sick of snow," Charles said.

"Me too," said Eva.

They stood looking from their family room at the mountains of snow, the layers of snow, the valleys of snow, the plateaus of snow. Snow made the windows white, the earth white; filled every nook, each cranny; sifted into every corner and crack and edge of the world. They had done all the sledding they could stand; all the snow forts they could build had been built: the first ten buried like Pompeii, the last five in degrees of backyard burial even as they watched. A thousand snowballs lay entombed: lumps of white coal waiting to be turned into diamonds by the crushing, building weight of snow.

Through the sliding glass door, only a thin line of gray sky could be seen at the top, above the geologic layers of snow.

And, in the gray sky, it snowed.

"I'm sick of snow," Eva said.

"So am I," said Charles.

They were weary of snow boots, of gloves and mittens; tired of tasseled hats and long johns and layers of socks; disgusted with dressing like astronauts each time they went out.

In the kitchen, where Mother and Father sat all but lifeless staring at their teacups, the radio called for more snow, crackled, went silent.

At the top of the sliding glass door, the last line of sky was filled in by snow, enclosing the world, making it go away.

"I'm *afraid* of snow," Charles said.

"Me too," Eva said.

And, in other places, other Charleses and other Evas said the same things.

Eva said: "Then we'll tunnel our way out."

"Yes!" said Charles.

They mounted their expedition like professionals.

Whistling, smiling, Charles rummaged through his room, through the cellar, through the attic. Eva organized. Charles loaded his arms with layers of socks and his book on Admiral Byrd. Eva piled up digging tools from the garage, the camping stove, Sterno cans for heat and cooking, and whatever was left to cook. She stuffed their school backpacks full with flashlight batteries and candy bars, comic books and automobile flares, boxes of matches, pots, and pans. In the pockets she put sunglasses against the glare, and her Walkman with tapes and Charles' lucky baseball card. She zipped the backpacks closed, afraid the straining seams would burst.

They dressed in their best clothes: ski parkas stuffed with goose feathers, snow pants with elastic straps to keep them in place. They had gloves with leatherette palms and fingers for gripping, crisp blue jeans, flannel lined. They wore two pairs of wool socks, gray and thick, and thermal underwear, and turtlenecks under sweatshirts that said 'Go Army!'

Outfitted and backpacked, they stood before the sliding glass door in the family room.

Eva looked at Charles, and Charles nodded.

Slowly, Eva unlocked the door, slid it back on its rails.

A wall of snow, smooth and white, high and wide, confronted them.

"Ready?" Eva said.

Charles said, "Ready."

They began to dig.

They dug.

And dug.

Scoop by scoop, handful by handful, Eva pushed snow back at Charles, who pushed it back into the room behind. A depression in the wall formed, kid-high and wide; the depression deepened and deepened until there was a little room made of snow, with snow walls, snow ceiling and snow floor, which they moved deeper into as they dug.

And dug.

And dug.

Charles looked back through their deepening tunnel. He saw the room they had left, the house they had left, far behind them, a shrinking cave opening.

And there—Mother and Father just glimpsed, beyond the family room piled with snow, heads lowered to the kitchen table, unmoving.

"Dig!" Eva ordered, and Charles turned away, taking Eva's handfuls of snow, her scoop and hand-shovelfuls of snow, packing them tight into the walls and ceiling and floor as they inched forward, onward.

Darkness deepened in their tunnel. Eva, panting in her snowsuit, stopped to hand Charles the big flashlight. Charles clicked it on. The walls gleamed blue-white. But already Eva was digging again, throwing snow back at Charles to pack away.

He lay the flashlight on the tunnel floor and went to work, inching the light forward.

Forward.

In the snow, on the floor under Eva's hand, something solid struck her fingers.

She brushed away snow, pushed away snow, packed away snow—and there beneath her lay a line of chicken wire across their path.

"Wha—?" Charles began.

"The fence!" Eva shouted. "It's the top of our backyard fence!"

And now Charles could imagine it, there beneath them in the far reaches of their yard, the line of wire tacked to posts.

Charles began, "That means—"

"We're four feet up!" Eva said.

They sat still, hushing their breathing.

Above them, far above, they heard the swishing of snow, the falling of snow.

"Keep digging!" Eva said.

"I'm tired!" Charles said. He lifted the flashlight, heavy in his hands, and shined it back behind them, where the light was lost in the far reaches of blue-white tunnel.

"We'll rest later!" Eva said, her own breath panting steam in the air.

Charles put the flashlight back down, pointed it at the wall of snow in front of them.

They dug.

And dug.

"Stop!" Eva said, breathing hard.

Charles dropped to the floor, leaned his back against the wall, let his arms drop like weights to his side.

"Tired . . ." he said.

Eva, still panting, brushed her heavy gloves one against the other, clearing them of snow. She reached into her pack and brought out candy bars and juice packs, potato chips and cookies.

Charles, gaining strength, began to eat, then drank. He ate everything she gave him.

"We don't have much more," Eva said, frowning.

Charles took the pack from her and dug in, finding more cookies.

"I'm hungry!" he said, ripping them open, letting Lorna Doones drop to the floor before he scooped them up.

Above them, snow swished and fell, brushed and fell, piled and fell.

* * *

After they began to dig again, the flashlight began to dim.

Almost at once, Eva's hand found something else solid in the floor.

She and Charles brushed and pushed snow away.

The edge of something square revealed itself.

"What—" Charles said.

Eva pushed more snow away, dug down and around, threw snow away with her fingers.

The corner of a box, steel with glass underneath—

"A phone booth!" Eva said.

She brushed more snow away, uncovered a sign with a bell on it, more glass below.

Charles shined the light down, saw the curve of a man's hat, the man slumped down, hand frozen to the dangling receiver, the man's face turned up toward him, *frozen*—

"Yahhhhh!" Charles said, scrambling back.

Eva took the flashlight, looked down into the booth herself.

"He's dead. Nothing we can do," she said, and immediately put the flash down again, aiming it ahead. "We're getting close to town."

She began to dig again, in the dimming light.

They left the phone booth behind. Soon they uncovered a telephone pole. They dug around it, leaving it standing straight and brown through the middle of their tunnel, creosote-smelling, with one steel footrest angled up like a pointing finger. They dug, and Eva's arms ached. Her fingers were numb with cold and work—but still she pushed and brushed and pulled at snow, raked it back at Charles who packed and pounded and beat and smoothed it into the walls and ceiling and floor. They felt the afternoon wear on, could feel the cold night coming, feel the snow falling, and sighing, and drifting, and soughing above them.

They dug.

And dug, and then Eva's nearly frozen fingers touched something solid beneath her, and she excavated around it.

She gasped, pulled her hand back.

The top of a head.

Black hair.

The flashlight was nearly out, a barely glowing bulb. She pulled it close, and Charles crawled up next to her.

Pushing more snow away, she uncovered a curve of feathers surrounding the head, rising in front to a war bonnet.

"Mr. Gray's wooden Indian!" she exclaimed.

Charles said, "We're in town! Next to the drugstore!"

Shaking the flashlight to make it brighten, they pushed the wall farther on. They dug and scraped and packed and bored, and soon hit the front of a store window, a wide plate of glass etched with Mr. Gray's name in large, arching letters.

GRAY'S
DRUG STORE

Pressing their cold faces to the glass, they looked down into the store.

There was blackness within.

"Darn!" Eva said, shaking the flashlight viciously, startled to find it go bright for her.

"Shine it inside!" Charles urged.

She directed the beam inside the drugstore. She played it over the soda fountain, over the glass cases, the prescription counter, the floor.

The beam fell on the dead figures of Mr. Gray, Mrs. Gray.

Eva turned the flashlight off. She and Charles lay in the dark, in the cold, listening to their own deep breaths and their own caught sobs.

Charles began to cry outright.

Eva smacked him with her gloved hand.

"Quiet!" she said.

"But I saw Mom, and Dad—"

"Yes!" Eva said.

"We might as well stay right here," Charles sniffled. "We might as well let it happen here. . . ."

Eva said nothing, listened to the snow above them, the snow falling.

Drifting.

Murmuring . . .

"No!" she said. "I won't give up!"

"We have no food, no light—nothing!"

"Dig!" Eva ordered, shaking the flashlight again and turning it on.

This time it only fluttered, a weak orange

glow, making the tunnel around them look like Halloween.

Charles sobbed, "I . . . can't . . ."

"Well I can!"

Eva began to bore up, angling away from the side of the drugstore.

She dropped handfuls of snow on Charles in the pumpkin light until he stopped crying and once more began to push and pack and pound.

They dug up.

Up.

Eva sensed the snow waiting for them. As she climbed she felt and heard it: the wash of snow, the gentle fall, the dusting and breathy blowing of snow. It reached out to her ears and heart, pulled her up toward its inevitable self. Behind her Charles sniffled and worked, inching the dying flashlight up with one hand while he pounded and smoothed with the other.

The flashlight went out; Halloween went away, leaving them with night.

Charles dropped the flashlight, listened to it slide down the steep tunnel like a sled until it was gone.

In the dark, they dug.

And dug.

And dug.

And then the wall of snow in front of Eva

suddenly went away: fell down around her in a shower leaving a hole.

The tunnel opened into dim light.

Eva and Charles climbed out onto the world.

It was snowing.

The planet was white. Snow drifted, twirled, and fell.

And fell; dropped in whispering breaths from the gray-white sky; shimmered pure and crystalline; fell fluffy and piled and moved like dust over the surface of the earth. From north to south, east to west, the world was white.

It snowed.

And snowed.

"Oh, Eva, what are we going to do!" said Charles, his eyes once more welling to tears.

Above them, the gray-white clouds darkened to gray.

Darkened still more.

Night was coming.

And it snowed.

"What—" Charles began, sobbing, but his sister took his arm and pointed.

"Look!"

There, through the drifting, swirling, gently lashing snow, was a dim point of light in the near distance.

"A star!" Charles said.

Eva took Charles' arm.

They tramped through the snow.

But now, the light began to stutter and die. Snow occluded it, and suddenly it was gone.

"No!" Charles cried.

The star blinked back on.

They hurried, and then they reached it: a star on the ground, a five-pointed lamp dimming, half buried by snow.

"Is it—" Charles said, but he knew what it was even as Eva began to brush snow away from it. She uncovered the top of the town Christmas tree, taller than any building.

Down there, under all the packed and piled and layered snow, was a huge branching evergreen tree with red bulbs and strings of fat lights and thick silver strands of tinsel.

The star flickered.

Went out.

Eva stood, and she and Charles watched as the snow drifted and accumulated and covered the top of the last point of the star.

To every horizon was snow; mountains and hills and valleys of snow.

Only snow.

"Oh, Eva! What are we going to do?" Charles said.

Eva looked at Charles and said, "I don't know."

Darkness fell.

It snowed.

* * *

And snowed.

Snow covered their tracks, drifting and sighing, swirling and filling. Eva and Charles wandered, flashlightless, freezing. Snow drifted and moved and mounted and fell in the dark-white world. The earth glowed dark blue-white, the air was a curtain of dark white.

It snowed.

On hands and knees, exhausted, they crawled until they could crawl no more.

"I . . . can't," Charles whispered, and stopped, turning over to sit in the snow.

Eva sat down beside him.

"Neither," she whispered, "can I."

She looked up, felt soft snow caress her cheeks, dance across her eyebrows, melt on her warm-cold nose.

"I wish it would stop snowing," Charles said.

Eva closed her eyes, felt snow tap on her face like fingers, slide down her cheeks, mingling with tears, which crystallized into snow.

"Me, too," she said. "I wish it would stop snowing."

There came a hush in the air.

Above, in the sky, Charles saw something that was not snow. A tiny light appeared in a tiny split of clouds. A swirl of falling snow blew aside and more tiny lights appeared.

"Stars!" Charles cried. "*Real* stars!"

Beside Charles and Eva there was a sound in

the snow. A sudden tunnel appeared. A bright stab of light shot out, followed by a mufflered boy bearing a flashlight.

Behind him came a snowsuited girl and another boy, all hat and scarf and ski jacket.

Other tunnels opened—a thousand tunnels, with other stabbing beams of light followed by other boys and girls.

"Look!" Charles shouted, pointing at the sky.

All over, flashlights were turned off and eyes were turned upward.

The night was full of stars and vanishing clouds.

It had stopped snowing.

In the night, by the light of the friendly moon, they brought up the world from below.

Through the tunnels, they carried up food and light and shelter. They brought up candy and juice packs and cookies and cake. They tunneled into empty Kmarts, carried up batteries by the boxful, chairs and tents and sleds and blankets. They brought up propane stoves and heaters, they brought up comic books and tape players and toys. They brought up more toys.

The starry night drained into rose dawn, and gave them day. They stood staring open-mouthed at the stranger Sun. They cheered as it climbed high into a cloudless firmament, cheered as it warmed their faces, made them throw off watch caps and ski masks and ear muffs and scarves. They cheered and sang and continued their work, toting up an entire new world from below.

In the golden afternoon Charles stood smiling, Eva beside him. He laughed at the sight of a forming puddle of melted snow.

"Maybe it'll all melt, right back down to the earth!"

"I hope," Eva shouted loud, *"it never snows again!"*

A cheer went up, everywhere.

In the sky, behind the sun, like a shy and peeking visitor, a thin cloud appeared, joined soon by others.

The skies darkened.

It began to snow.

Sure, you hate homework. Everyone does. But did you ever wonder how your homework feels about you?

THE HOMEWORK HORROR

Greg Cox

Danny giggled as he did his homework.

Marjorie Schweiker shook her head. Sometimes she just didn't understand her son. What was so funny about third-grade math? Across from her, on the other side of a bright red kitchen table, Danny had his nose just a few inches away from a sheet of problems. A full mug of Nestle's Chocolate sat ignored beside a huge rubber eraser. He looked so cute, Marjorie thought, with that "I'm-concentrating-so-hard" expression on his face. He put down his pencil, but only long enough to count up and down on his fingers. "Take that, number five!" he muttered, then giggled again.

"Having some fun, eh kiddo?" Marjorie asked.

Danny shrugged without looking up.

"You know, when I was your age I hated

math. All those numbers seemed really boring. Not that I'm complaining about you working so hard on your schoolwork; that's neat. I'm proud of you, just confused."

"Nothing confusing to me, Mom. Numbers aren't boring if you understand who they are."

"*Who* they are?"

"Yeah. All the problems are like stories, and the numbers are the people."

"Uh, right. Whatever you say." Marjorie got up and gave the kid a friendly hair-mussing on her way to the living room of their duplex apartment. "Just keep up the good work, sport." Crossing the carpet, she cleared off a space on the couch and reached for the *TV Guide.*

Danny leaned back, carefully balancing the chair on its two rear legs. A big gulp of chocolate milk went down his throat. Somehow, he realized, he had failed to convince his mother.

It was true, though. Numbers had personalities just like people. Except for zero, of course, which was nothing. Big numbers were always stronger than little numbers, just like odd numbers were more emotional than the even ones. There were nine different characters in all, each special in its own way.

One was the smallest and kind of dull; he couldn't do very much. Two was a friendly number, but weak also. Three was an okay guy, but unpredictable and not too smart (kind of like the big kids at recess). Four was very wise and very mellow. And then there was five.

Danny skipped quickly to the next number.

Six was one of the good guys, but not quite grown-up yet. Poor six! He was always going to be outclassed by his big brother seven, the greatest number of them all. Seven was a real hero, who managed to combine the best qualities of both odd and even numbers. You could always trust seven.

Not like five, Danny thought despite himself.

Then there were eight and nine, the rulers of the number line. The king and his counselor. Eight was a mysterious genius, and second only to the aloof and powerful number nine. Nine belonged with the good guys, but he was also what Danny's mother called "an authority figure" and naturally a little scary.

All in all, Danny liked most of the numbers. Except five.

You could tell just by looking at five that she was the bad one in the bunch. There she sat in the middle of the number line, within striking distance of either end, coiled up on her bottom curve like a cobra about to attack. Danny had no doubts at all. Five was evil.

The red metal chair fell forward and Danny reached for his pencil. He looked at his assignment: rows of black numbers covering a field of white paper. There was only one more problem left to solve, one more battle between the numbers. One more chance to add, subtract, multiply, and divide wicked old five into nonexistence.

Danny grinned bloodthirstily. This had been a good night. He'd slaughtered five so many times that he almost felt guilty about it.

A little while later, Danny carried the rolled-up problem sheet to his mother on the couch.

"I'm all finished, Mom. You want to check my answers?"

"Sure, kiddo. Let me see."

Usually it took his mom a couple of minutes to proofread his homework, so Danny figured he had time to go get a comic book from his room. He didn't think he would have to do any of the problems over. Mom almost never found any mistakes in his mathwork, only in his spelling. Still, she liked to check everything, so he let her.

But when he came back to the room, Danny saw that his mother was frowning.

"Sorry," she said, "but you must not have been concentrating as hard as I thought. All your answers are wrong."

Danny couldn't believe it. "All of them?"

"Yep. You'd better get back to the table and look at these again. And leave the comic book here."

Once in the kitchen again, Danny stared at the pairs of tiny violet numbers. He didn't recognize any of them. This was the same sheet he had given to his mom, those were his answers written in pencil, but the problems themselves were different than he remembered. It was as if all the numbers had moved across the page when nobody was looking, rearranging themselves into new combinations. But that didn't make sense. Numbers were too well-behaved to pull stunts like that. Most numbers were, at least.

It was weird.

As much as he enjoyed playing with numbers, Danny resented having to do the same homework twice, sort of. He scowled and angrily blew all the air out of his cheeks, rustling the top of the paper, and put his eraser to work destroying all the old answers. Then, when the last grey line was gone, he started counting on his fingers again.

After the first ten problems, he was trembling.

The new answers were what freaked him out: 55, 505, 50005, 50. And so on. Immediately, he re-checked all his calculations, looking for mistakes and not finding any. Had he carried the one over here? Yes. Did eight minus three really equal that? Yes. What was one plus four again?

Help, he thought. *Number five has taken over my homework.*

Danny tried to finish the page, as quickly as possible.

Five—just five—was the answer to the *next* ten problems.

Danny felt close to tears. "Mom?" he called. "Can I quit for a while? Please! I'll do the rest in the morning, I promise."

"Oh, okay," replied his mother's voice. "Guess we don't want you to burn out at age nine. Take a break."

Uncharacteristically quiet, Danny crept out of the kitchen, looking over his shoulder all the time at the thin sheet of paper that was now The Scene of the Crime. No matter how hungry he got, Danny vowed, he wasn't going to enter the kitchen again until breakfast. This time of year it got dark early, and he wasn't going to chance being caught alone with haunted homework after nightfall. Evil things, like five, did their best work after dark.

He wished he hadn't thought of that, because now he couldn't help wondering what was going to happen next. Maybe five was only teasing him now, and the worst stuff came later. Danny sat down in the hall and punched the floor with his fist. *No fair,* he thought. *Why me?*

He knew why. Five was mad at him because of all the times Danny had calculated her to death. He had enjoyed it too much and now five was getting even. But how mad was five?

"Stop it," Danny said to himself. He did not want to think about it anymore. He would

watch TV instead. The hallway led to the stairs, and the stairs went to the second floor where Danny's bedroom was. He ran the entire route and shut the door behind him, then locked it with a short length of brass-plated chain. Only after Danny ensured that the door was secure did he kick away some of the general clutter and drop to his knees in front of his own black-and-white TV set. Because Mom was around, he turned on the educational channel. *Sesame Street* was just ending.

The closing credits were rolling over a frozen close-up of Big Bird. Danny heard an invisible announcer speaking: "—thiss episssode wass brought to you by the number five and the letters D-I-E—"

Danny's arm snapped forward and switched off the television. Hugging himself, he backed away from the now-empty screen. The announcer's voice—it was different! Colder than usual, and hissing, sort of. Like a cobra.

Now he was truly scared, scared for his life. Five was out to get him for real. But what could he do? Who would protect him? Mom didn't understand; she hadn't believed him before. Dad lived on the other side of the country now, but, even if he were here, Danny didn't think he could explain the danger to his father. Grown-ups just laughed at monsters like five. Even when they were real.

There were no other children he could call.

Danny was new in town and school had only started about a week ago. All his best friends were still imaginary.

Still, maybe if he just stayed near Mom . . .

Danny headed for the living room, only to meet his mother on the stairs. She was wearing her jacket and slipping on a pair of winter gloves. "Ah, there you are," she said. "I just wanted to tell you that I was stepping out for a sec. I've got to run down the road and pay some bills before the post office closes. Try not to burn the building down while I'm gone."

Danny worked hard to control his fear. He did not want to be left alone. Not now.

"Mom, wait! Let me go with you."

She shook her head. "Sorry, kid, but I'm in a hurry. Let me do this trip on my own, okay? It'll be faster that way." She untangled her purse from the stairway railing and headed for the front door. His face must have given away some of his distress, because she paused on the porch. "Hey, it's no big deal. I'll be real quick. You'll just have to manage by yourself for a few minutes. At most, five."

The door clicked shut, trapping Danny inside.

Alone for five minutes. Five. Danny hated the sound of that. He gazed up at the wooden cuckoo clock over the door. The time was 5:50. In five minutes, probably just before Mom got back, it would be 5:55. The very moment when that horrible, revenge-crazed number would be strongest.

This was it, Danny thought. His last stand. If only he could just last till six o'clock, he would be safe. Six was a good number and kind towards helpless little boys who didn't mean any harm.

Suddenly, a loud crash came from below, like a metal chair hitting the floor. The noise sounded like it came from the kitchen, where Danny had left his homework unwatched and unguarded. *Something* was moving down there.

Danny moved too. He ran back into his room, then threw himself against the door to close it. Frantic, he fumbled with the brass chain, terrified that something awful would push the door open before he finished locking it out. "Something awful?" *Ha ha ha,* Danny thought. Deep down inside, he already knew what was downstairs. His imagination brought him a vivid picture of the number five, as tall as Danny or bigger, rising up from the flat whiteness of the math paper, knocking over a chair in the process.

Even after the chain was safely in place between the door and the adjoining wall, he pressed himself tightly against the door. His ears strained to catch any new noises from the rest of the apartment. At first he didn't hear anything, then . . . there! What was that? Danny was sure he heard a sound at the bottom of the stairs, a low unbroken whistling, a long steady hiss that grew louder every second as it came up the stairs, getting closer and closer to the bedroom door.

Something scratched at the other side of the wood.

Danny jumped backwards. He looked around desperately. What did you fight an angry number with? His plastic clock-radio, a gift from Danny's last (and maybe *final*) birthday, sat on top of an aluminum toy chest. The lighted, green figures on its digital display read 5:53 P.M.

Two more minutes to go before the horror struck. Danny closed his eyes and tried to summon up reinforcements. Not nine or eight, the undisputed masters of the numbers. They would not concern themselves with the problems of a mere human boy. No, Danny clenched his fists and tried to picture seven in his mind. Seven, the Sir Lancelot of arithmetic! Only he could save the day, Danny thought.

But even his own imagination seemed to have turned against him. With both eyes tightly shut, Danny could see the shape of seven—two straight lines joined at an angle—but he could not hold it still. The figure kept spinning in his mind, turning head-over-heels like a pinwheel, and finally came to a stop *on its side.* That wasn't right at all. Danny could not see a seven anymore, only the letter V.

"Oh no!" he gasped. Instantly, Danny opened

his eyes and pushed the picture out of his head. *That was a close call,* he thought. Danny knew about Roman numerals.

Seven was not going to be able to help him. He was on his own this time. *Oh Mom,* he mourned silently, *why did you have to leave?*

Then, through the crack between the door and the wall, five slid into the room. Danny saw her and let out a small cry. Five looked like a shadow on the white, painted surface of his bedroom walls, but darker than an ordinary shadow: a deep menacing black. Five was long and thin, with a jagged outline, and resembled a heavy, twisted cable smashed flat. She hissed as she moved.

Five circled Danny, gliding from wall to wall to wall. Standing in the center of a litter-strewn carpet, Danny spun on his toes, trying to keep the huge numerical invader in sight.

It was 5:54.

Danny's heel slipped on a scrap of paper and he almost fell. Without thinking, he glanced down at the floor. Something golden and glittery caught his eye; he recognized it right away. It was a foil star affixed to one of his old report cards. Danny remembered the star. His first-grade teacher had placed it there, under a column labeled "Math Skills."

Five moved closer. Danny bent quickly and plucked the crumpled report card from the carpet. New confidence filled him. "See this star!"

he shouted. "It means that I'm an A-One math whiz. You can't scare me. You're just another number and I can make numbers do anything I want."

Five backed off, sliding onto the wall farthest from her intended victim. Danny kept the card between him and the vengeful number, brandishing it at arm's length like the hero in a vampire movie holds his cross. Light from a bulb overhead reflected off the sparkling star, and golden beams danced around the room. Five stayed in the shadows and kept her distance.

Until 5:55.

At that moment, as soon as the numbers on the digital clock changed over, five slid down the wall and onto the floor. Before Danny could move, five's curved tail hooked around his feet and pulled shut. Barbed-wire teeth stabbed him through his socks. Danny's body jerked. He dropped the report card. The radiator suddenly clicked on and newborn air currents blew the card, complete with its shiny little sticker, all the way across the room.

Five tightened her grip, grinding Danny's ankles together painfully. Even as he cried out, though, he refused to surrender. He could still see his golden star. Five was not in charge here, Danny knew, not as long as he could still remember how to add.

With his small right hand, Danny grabbed

the giant five by her single vertical bar, then stood up, partially dragging the hissing number from the plane of the floor. He reached for the clock-radio with his other hand. It was still slightly too far away. Without letting go of five, Danny stretched his arm until a few fingers just grazed the clock's plastic face. He held his breath and tried to visualize a plus sign between the five and the clock.

For a second, he really saw it: two crossed bars of intangible light hanging before his eyes. Then a momentary flash of green to the left of his head attracted him. Danny turned and saw the numbers of the digital clock jump instantly from 5:55 to 6:00 P.M.

Five's jagged tail loosened and pulled away, and Danny kicked his feet apart. He felt five's thin neck shrink between his fingers. Downstairs, the cuckoo clock released the first of a half-dozen enthusiastic chirps.

Danny gave his clock a friendly pat. "Way to go, little six. You did good!"

The glowing green number flickered once, as if to agree.

Marjorie Schweiker heard all the cuckooing as she came onto the porch outside her apartment. *That's odd,* she thought. Had she really been away that long? Oh well, it probably didn't matter. That was the problem with people today. Slaves of the clock.

Marjorie unlocked the front door and stepped inside. "Danny? You survive after all?"

"I guess so," came the answer from up the stairway. A moment later, she saw her boy tramping down the steps. He was breathing hard, she noticed, and limping slightly. One hand stayed behind his back. A sharpened pencil hung from a belt-loop at his side, like a sword dangling upon the waist of some heroic warrior of old. He had something stuck in the middle of his forehead. A tiny paper star, it looked like.

"What in the world are you playing now?" she asked. "What's that sticker on your forehead for—and how did you tear up the cuffs of your pants?"

But Danny would not stop to explain anything. "In a minute, Mom," he said and hurried past her. He kept his hand hidden away, but Marjorie caught a glimpse of something dark and wiry twisting about in her son's fist.

"Wait!" she said and started after him, though Danny had already disappeared into the kitchen. Marjorie made it halfway there, but was stopped cold by an angry sibilant scream, followed by a barrage of pounding noises.

"What the—?" she began.

HISSS—WHACK, WHACK!

The noises stopped. Danny emerged from the kitchen with pencil in hand. There was a weary-but-triumphant smile on his face.

"I finished off my homework, Mom."

And with that, he thrust his No. 2 pencil into his belt and marched up the stairs.

Today, arithmetic. Tomorrow, spelling tests.

What are friends for?

BLACKWATER DREAMS

Tim Waggoner

Aaron was swimming in the middle of a vast body of water which stretched endlessly in all directions. He would have thought it an ocean had the water been salty. However, it was fresh water, and that meant a lake. But it was the biggest lake he had ever seen in his life.

The sky was purple-gray with a hint of fading orange off in the distance—dusk. Night would fall soon, and that meant Aaron would be swimming in darkness. He didn't like that. How would he ever find the shore if he couldn't see where he was going? Not, he told himself, that it would matter. He couldn't see the shore now, could he? He began swimming in the direction of the light, for no other reason than that it was a way to go, and he couldn't expect to get to the shore by treading water.

The lake was cold. Not ice-cold, but a subtle cold. The kind that stole warmth from the body slowly, bit by bit, until before you knew it, your limbs were numb and heavy and you couldn't make them keep pulling you through the water. Aaron forced himself not to think about the cold and the approaching darkness. Instead, he thought of drying off before a warm, cozy, safe campfire. But he still felt the water's cold seeping through his skin.

Aaron wasn't the world's greatest swimmer, and before long he found himself beginning to tire. The cold, and his lack of practice, were taking their toll. His lungs ached and his muscles burned. But still he kept moving his arms and legs, stroke after stroke, for if he didn't, he knew what would happen, knew he would sink, would drown. Would die.

Still no hint of shore in sight, and what little light there had been was nearly gone.

Aaron.

He told himself that he hadn't heard the watery whisper, that it was just his imagination, or fatigue.

Aaron . . .

Adrenaline shot through him and the pain in his muscles momentarily faded. He surged through the water like a torpedo, desperate to put distance between himself and the voice.

Aaron! Louder now, far more than a whisper, almost a shout. *Wait!* And Aaron felt a slimy cold something—something that felt an awful lot like a hand—brush his foot.

He screamed.

Aaron woke with a start. He was covered in sweat, sweat that smelled a lot like lake water. His heart pounded and his lungs heaved, and he sat up in bed and waited for them to calm down. When his pulse and breathing were closer to normal, he looked at the alarm clock on his night stand. He would have to get up for school in another eighteen minutes.

He knew he wouldn't be able to go back to sleep in the time he had. Rather than lie in bed and stare at the ceiling, he decided he might as well start getting ready. He got out of bed, put on his robe, and headed down the hall toward the bathroom, careful to walk quietly so he wouldn't wake up his parents or his six-year-old sister Bridgett.

He turned on the bathroom light and looked at himself in the mirror. He immediately wished he hadn't. His eyes were red, with big dark circles under them. Maybe a shower would help. He turned on the water and waited until it was nice and hot—the exact opposite of the murky water in his dream—before taking off his robe and getting in.

Despite the water's warmth, he shivered when it first struck his body. Even though it was warm, it was still water, and after what had happened last year—almost a year ago to the day—Aaron didn't like water.

As he picked up the soap and began to wash himself, the memory came back to him again.

He and his best friend Donnie were eleven, and their parents, who were all friends too, had decided to rent a cottage on Lake Blackwater for the weekend. It was the beginning of May and school was nearly over, so Aaron and Donnie had thought of the trip as a kind of prevacation, a way to kick off the summer and get it started right. They fished and boated with their families, explored the woods around the lake on their own, and just generally had a good time messing around.

But come Saturday night, Donnie was bored. After Bridgett and Donnie's five-year-old sister Margaret were put to bed, the parents wanted to sit around a campfire and roast marshmallows and talk, and while Aaron didn't mind this so much—actually kind of liked it, in fact, although he never would have admitted it to Donnie—the idea made Donnie nuts.

"I can't think of anything worse than sitting around a fire listening to our folks tell stupid stories and make a bunch of dumb jokes!" he'd said.

Aaron asked Donnie if he had a better idea.

Donnie grinned. "You bet I do!"

Donnie wanted to sneak down to the lake, "borrow" the rowboat Aaron's dad had brought, and do a little fishing. "We'll tell them we're just going for a walk or something. They'll be having so much fun talking that they won't notice us sneak out our fishing gear."

Aaron was uneasy about using his dad's boat without permission, but Donnie said they'd take good care of it, and besides, his dad would never know. Aaron wasn't sure. He was afraid they'd get caught, but Donnie had been his best friend since they were five, and he always found a way out of everything. So, in the end, Aaron said okay.

They made their excuse, sneaked out their fishing gear, and headed down to the dock. Once in the boat, they untied the knot of rope that anchored it to the dock, and rowed out onto the lake, taking turns at the oars.

Aaron put on one of the life jackets his dad kept under the seats, but Donnie refused. He said they were for people who weren't good swimmers, and since he was a great swimmer, he didn't need one. Aaron didn't argue; he knew there was no use when it came to Donnie.

Once Donnie decided they were out far enough, they dropped the anchor, baited their hooks by flashlight and cast their lines.

It took a little while, but Donnie got the first bite.

There was a strong tug on the line, and they knew it was a big fish. Donnie whooped in excitement, hauled back on his pole, and started to reel it in. But the fish was strong and resisted, so Donnie stood up to get into a better position.

"Hey, be careful!" Aaron said.

"Shut up! I know what I'm doing!"

But as Donnie struggled to reel in the fish, the boat started rocking. Aaron gripped the sides and said, "You better sit down before . . ."

He was too late. Donnie lost his balance and fell into the lake. There was a loud splash and a sickening thump. The boat rocked and nearly capsized.

"Donnie!" Aaron called. He waited for his friend to bob to the surface, cursing the fish that had caused him to get a dunking. But there was no sign of him. Fear cut through Aaron. What if that thump had been Donnie hitting his head against the boat as he fell? What if he was knocked out and couldn't swim?

"Donnie!" he yelled. "Where are you?"

No answer.

Aaron stood and jumped into the lake, his life jacket keeping him afloat. He thrashed about, calling Donnie's name over and over, praying that he'd feel his friend's hand grab his, but all he felt was empty water. Donnie was gone.

The authorities dragged the lake for Donnie's body, but it was never found. Aaron's parents had been too upset over Donnie's death to punish him, but it wouldn't have mattered if they

had. No punishment could have been worse than losing his best friend.

That had been a year ago. And ever since Aaron didn't want anything to do with water. He hadn't set foot in a swimming pool, wouldn't take a bath, didn't even like when it rained. A shower was as much as he was willing to endure, and then only because the water came out in thin, warm streams and vanished down the drain. Even so, he took very quick showers.

And then there were the dreams. They'd begun a couple months ago, with Aaron stranded in the middle of an endless lake, desperately swimming for a shore that wasn't there. The dreams had stayed the same for a while, but lately a new element had been added. A voice. Donnie's voice, calling to him. And then last night, another change—the cold fingers reaching for him.

Donnie's fingers.

The next night, Aaron had the same dream. Again he was swimming in the lake, the sun almost down, the water cold. Again he heard the voice and felt those frigid, wet fingers brush against his foot. Only this time they nearly got a grip.

He awoke the same way he had the night before, drenched in sweat, gasping for breath.

But this time, when he got out of bed, his feet came down on a wet patch in the carpet.

Aaron jumped off the wetness, a shiver running down his back. He hesitated, then bent and touched his fingers to the wet area. He brought them up to his nose and sniffed. He'd never forget that smell; it was the brackish odor of Lake Blackwater.

His first thought was that Donnie had been here. His second thought was that he was crazy. He didn't know which possibility frightened him more.

It started to sprinkle when Aaron got on the bus that afternoon to go home, and by the time he reached his stop, it was raining hard. Aaron hesitated before stepping off the bus; he didn't want to go out into the rain, didn't want to feel the clammy water against his skin. But he was aware of the bus driver watching him, not to mention the other kids, so he took a deep breath and dashed into the rain.

Despite the time of year, the rain was cold and coming down so fast that the drops stung like bee stings. Aaron was soaked to the skin before he had taken three steps.

There was so much rain falling that his house was only a hazy gray blur before him. But he kept running toward the dry safety of his porch, his footing uncertain on the slippery grass. He was struck by how much like his dream this was: he was wet, cold, and surrounded by water on all sides, desperately trying to get to shore—or in this case, to his porch. All that was missing was . . .

Aaron.

The voice.

Aaron!

Donnie's voice. Coming from behind him.

Wait up!

Aaron felt a strong urge to turn around and see what, if anything, was there behind him. Instead he poured on the speed and reached the porch steps. With two large bounds he was up on the porch itself, safe, safe.

Don't leave me, Aaron!

He did turn then, and what he saw made his blood freeze in his veins. In the middle of the yard, coming toward him, was the watery outline of a human figure, as if whatever was there couldn't be seen by the naked eye, could only be detected by the rainwater that clung to its surface.

The figure took several more steps toward the porch, its arms outstretched, liquidy hands reaching, reaching . . .

Aaron wanted to turn and run inside, wanted at the very least to scream, but his body wouldn't listen. All he could do was stand and watch as the figure came closer.

It reached the porch and set a foot on the first step, and then, after a moment's hesitation, on the second. Then, out of the rain, the figure shuddered and collapsed, its liquid substance splashing onto the steps and running down to merge with the puddles pooling in the yard.

Aaron stood trembling, staring at the spot where the watery apparition had been, his nostrils filled with the stink of wet decay.

Aaron spent the rest of the afternoon in his room. He lay on the bed and stared at the ceiling, trying to puzzle out what was going on.

Tomorrow would be exactly a year since Donnie drowned. Aaron asked himself if he was feeling guilty because he hadn't been able to save his best friend—so guilty he had been having those terrible dreams, dreams which had started to spill over into the waking world. Or was it possible that somehow Donnie's spirit really was reaching out to him? Maybe Donnie was angry that Aaron hadn't done more to save him. Maybe he wanted to get even.

Aaron shook his head and told himself he was being stupid. Things like that only happened in the movies. His parents had made him see a psychologist after Donnie had died, and she'd said it was only natural for him to feel some guilt, and that it would take a while before he learned to live with what had happened. Obviously that was all that was going on. The anniversary of Donnie's death was approaching and he was just having trouble dealing with it, that was all. When it was over, his life would return to normal.

He rolled onto his side and reached down to touch the spot on the carpet that had been wet this morning.

Guilt or no guilt, it was still damp.

Aaron finally left his room when his mother called him downstairs for dinner. He ate without tasting anything, and he answered his parents' questions about school as briefly as he thought they'd let him get away with. Bridgett tried to irritate him by making faces when their folks weren't looking, but when she saw that Aaron was ignoring her, she quit and pouted.

Aaron's mother turned to his father. "You know, Ray, the strangest thing happened today."

"Hmmm?" his dad replied.

"I was vacuuming this afternoon after work and I came across this wet patch of carpet in the upstairs hallway."

Aaron felt frost gathering on his spine.

"I didn't do it!" Bridgett said automatically.

"I know you didn't, sweetheart," his mom responded. "The hall was dry when you and Aaron left for school."

"It rained hard this afternoon," Dad said. "Maybe we've got a leak in the roof."

"I checked. The ceiling was dry. Besides, this happened before the rain got bad."

Dad shrugged. "Who knows? I'll call somebody and have them come over and check it out."

Aaron didn't need anyone else to tell him what had happened. He had a pretty good idea.

Normally after dinner Aaron would've gone back up to his room to do his homework. But tonight he didn't want to be alone, so he sat on the floor in the family room and watched TV with his dad while Mom played a board game with Bridgett.

At 7:30, Aaron's mom took Bridgett upstairs to get her bath started. Bridgett was old enough to take a bath by herself, and she often stayed in the tub for a whole half hour, playing with her toys and dolls. Aaron used to do the same when he was little, and he longed for the time when being in the water had been simple fun.

After a bit, Mom came back downstairs, sat on the couch and started to relax. A moment later, Bridgett screamed.

His mother sprang up and ran for the stairs, his father close behind. Aaron sat paralyzed for a moment before he too finally jumped up and followed them.

When he got to the bathroom he saw Bridgett, wrapped in a fuzzy white towel, being held and rocked by Mom. Dad stood by, concern and worry all over his face.

"There was something in the water with

me!" Bridgett sobbed. Tears rolled down her face and she could barely get the words out through her shuddering, gasping breaths. "It tried to grab my foot!"

Aaron turned and walked out of the bathroom. He knew now what he had to do.

It took a while, but eventually Mom was able to calm Bridgett down and get her to go to sleep. Aaron lay on his bed again, the light on, and thought about what would soon happen, what must happen.

It seemed Donnie wasn't picky about how he had his revenge. If he couldn't get Aaron he would go after Aaron's family. No matter how scared he was, Aaron couldn't let that happen. His family hadn't done anything. They hadn't been the ones to lie about going for a walk that night at Lake Blackwater, hadn't been the ones unable to save their friend's life. He was the one responsible, and if there was any price to be paid, he would be the one to pay it.

He turned off the light and waited for sleep—and whatever else—to come.

The dream began, and Aaron found himself in the middle of the gigantic lake. But instead of swimming frantically toward a distant and perhaps nonexistent shore, he took a deep breath, closed his eyes, and dove beneath the waves.

He swam down, down, listening for Donnie's voice, knowing he wouldn't have long to wait.

Aaron! The voice was strong and clear despite reaching his ears through water. Donnie was nearby.

Aaron stopped swimming. *Do whatever you want with me,* he thought, knowing that Donnie would be able to understand him, for anything was possible in dreams. *I'm ready to pay.*

And then Aaron heard something which surprised him: Donnie's laughter.

I don't want you to pay for anything, stupid. You're my best friend—I want you to come with me. I've got so much to show you.

Aaron couldn't believe it. *But you tried to drown me here in the dream lake, and when that didn't work, you came after me in the real world! And when you couldn't get me, you went after Bridgett!*

I wasn't trying to hurt you or your sister, Donnie thought. *I was just trying to get your attention. It sure took long enough.*

Aaron could feel the smile behind Donnie's words, and he knew his friend was telling the truth.

Relieved, Aaron opened his eyes. Despite the inky blackness of the water, he was able to make out Donnie's features just fine, and he could see the smile he had only sensed a moment ago.

And he realized that Donnie didn't blame him for what had happened.

That's right, I don't. And what's more, you shouldn't blame yourself either. It was just an accident. Okay?

Another smile, one that Aaron returned.

Okay.

Good, Donnie thought. *Now let's go.* He held out his hand.

Aaron hesitated, afraid. He had no idea where Donnie intended to lead him, what he wanted Aaron to see. But Donnie was his friend, and Aaron knew now that he would never hurt him. He put his fear aside, and reached out and took Donnie's hand.

As Donnie led him down into the darkness, Aaron wondered if next morning he would wake from this dream, or if his family would come to check on him only to find a puddle of lake water slowly drying on the sheets. He supposed he would find out soon enough.

Together, he and Donnie continued downward, toward the terrible, wonderful secrets far below.

Sometimes saying goodbye is the hardest thing of all.

AMANDA'S ROOM

Janni Lee Simner

Wind moaned through the room, rattling the blinds, tearing my posters right off the walls. It blew my scrapbooks from the desk, my books from the shelves, a full glass of water from the dresser. The glass shattered, but the wind went on, spraying water all around and whistling fiercely, as if looking for something. Looking for me.

"Stop it!" I hid beneath my knitted yellow bedspread, though the summer night was warm and sweat dripped down the back of my neck. The wind pulled hard at the blanket, trying to tear it away. "Amanda!" I screamed. "Leave me alone!"

At the sound of my yell, Mom's footsteps echoed down the hall. I heard her pull the bedroom door open. As she did the wind stopped, as if it had never been there at all.

"Brenda, what is it? What's wrong?"

I poked my head out to see Mom standing over my bed. Books and papers were scattered everywhere, along with shards of sharp glass. Water dripped from the dresser, but otherwise the room was perfectly silent.

Mom and Dad never heard Amanda. Only me.

Mom shook her head, seeing only the mess my room had become. "That's the third time this week, Brenda. I know you're not comfortable sleeping in your sister's old room yet, but throwing tantrums isn't the answer. Not when you're nearly twelve."

I pulled the blankets back up to my chin. "It's not a tantrum," I said, though I knew Mom wouldn't believe me. I'd tried explaining before.

Amanda didn't want me in her room.

She never had. Even before she'd gotten sick, she'd always complained I was in the way, yelled at me for touching her things, dragged Mom and Dad in to make me keep out. As if somehow just by being there I was ruining all her stuff. The only time she hadn't cared what I did was that last awful month, when she'd lain pale and tired in the hospital bed. But I tried not to think about that. Tried so hard that sometimes it was all I did think about.

"Maybe—" I began, tentatively, without much hope, "maybe I should just move back into my old room." I'd never wanted to move,

and three weeks had done nothing to change that.

Mom moved one hand to her stomach, though I couldn't see the baby that was coming, not yet. "You know your dad and I have already begun redecorating," she said, though I doubted it would matter if they hadn't started. Mom and Dad wanted the baby in the room next to theirs, so they could keep an eye on it. Just like they'd kept an eye on me when I was a baby, and on Amanda before me.

I swallowed. They could have kept an eye on Amanda all her life, and that wouldn't have been enough to save her.

Mom sighed. "I know it's hard, honey. But I'm sure Amanda would understand."

She was wrong about that. Amanda and I had never understood each other, not really. Mom claims we were close when we were little, but all I can remember is how we were always fighting, about all sorts of stupid stuff—my going into Amanda's room, Amanda trying to switch the TV station halfway through a show, who got the front seat when Mom or Dad drove us somewhere. We fought about who was smarter, who Mom and Dad liked best, whose fault it was we were fighting. Even after Amanda got sick, we couldn't seem to stop. If anything, the fighting only got worse.

Mom didn't seem to remember that, though. Dad neither. They suddenly seemed to think

Amanda had been perfect all her life. It was as if when Amanda died, she'd somehow taken the memories of all the bad stuff away. Except she'd forgotten to take them from me.

Mom leaned down and kissed me gently on the forehead. "It's been six months, Brenda. We need to start moving forward."

I didn't answer. Mom had been talking about moving forward since the day after Amanda died, but I know she didn't believe her own words. If she did, what was she having another baby for? She and Dad talked a lot about their "unexpected surprise" lately, but I wasn't stupid. I knew they were doing this on purpose, that they thought everything would somehow be all right once they had two kids again.

My throat tightened; I avoided Mom's weary gaze. I might not have always liked Amanda much, but that didn't mean I wanted some other kid around instead.

Mom sighed again. "Just try and get some sleep, okay? You can clean this mess up in the morning."

"Yeah," I told her. "Sure."

Mom tucked the blankets in around me, just like she had when I was much smaller. As she walked back into the hall, I thought I heard her crying.

My throat still hurt, but my own eyes were dry. If someone wasn't moving forward, I thought fiercely, it wasn't me.

I didn't think I'd be able to sleep, but eventually I must have dozed off, because I woke to a low moaning whistle. No wind this time, just Amanda's voice whispering, "Get out of my room. Get out of my room," over and over. The words were cold as ice; they scraped against my bones like fingernails on a blackboard. I dug my nails into my palms, bit my lip so hard it bled, but the scraping wouldn't go away. Even dead, my sister wouldn't leave me alone.

"Get out of my room. Get out of my room."

Her voice grew louder and colder, until I knew that if I listened any longer I'd start screaming. I grabbed my blanket, shoved my feet into my slippers, and fled to the living room, huddling deep into the couch.

But even when I finally fell back asleep, Amanda's voice followed me, echoing deep into my dreams.

Mom and Dad were furious when they found me on the couch the next day, but they both had to leave for work, so there wasn't much they could do. It was summer, and I didn't have to go anywhere, so I slept a while longer after they left. This time Amanda didn't bother me. I didn't wake until midmorning, when the room had turned sticky and hot. I stumbled up to turn on the air-conditioning then, my skin damp with sweat, eyelids gritty and stiff. I felt like I'd hardly slept at all that night. Like I'd hardly slept at all since moving into Amanda's room.

I couldn't stay there, no matter what Mom and Dad said. I had to give Amanda her room back. It was the only way I could think of to make her leave me alone. I'd tried everything else, yelling at her and hiding from her and ignoring her. Nothing worked.

I pulled on shorts and a T-shirt and went out to the garage, where Mom and Dad had boxed up all Amanda's things. I dragged the boxes into her room, and one by one, I started unpacking them. Maybe when Mom and Dad saw all Amanda's stuff out in that room, they'd realize I was right, that those things belonged there—and that I didn't belong there.

I took my yellow blanket off the bed and replaced it with Amanda's pale blue quilt. I pulled my adventure books off the shelves—those that hadn't already been knocked down—and replaced them with Amanda's romances. I boxed up my scrapbooks and put out Amanda's journals. Even my posters (mostly of cute guys) came down, and Amanda's (of guys who weren't so cute) went up instead. Along the way I cleaned up all the broken glass and water and the rest of the mess from the night before.

All the while I did this, no wind blew, no blinds shook, no voice whistled through the room. Instead the air grew quieter and quieter, the sounds from outside all fading away, until

I could hear my own breath, moving in and out of my lungs. The silence deepened, making me want to yell, to scream, to run from Amanda's room and never go back. Instead I kept unpacking. I had to finish this now, before Mom and Dad got home.

The room turned colder and colder, too. I flipped the air conditioner off. The rest of the house became hot and steamy, but Amanda's room stayed as icy as a refrigerator. Goose bumps rose on my bare arms and legs.

And when I finished unpacking and stepped back to look the room over, I felt even colder.

The posters were battered from having been taken down and put up again, and the books weren't in quite the right order, but otherwise what I saw really could have been Amanda's old room. Yet something was wrong. Maybe it was just that everything looked too neat and ordered from having just been unpacked. Maybe it was how quiet the room still was.

Maybe it was that Amanda's stuff was all there, but Amanda wasn't.

"You can have your room back now!" My voice cut through the silence, but no one answered, not a sound. "That's what you wanted, isn't it?" Still no answer, even though last night I couldn't make her go away. Yet now— I'd been so sure Amanda would come back, once all her things were here.

So sure she'd come back.

Until that moment I hadn't known, hadn't wanted to know, the real reason I'd brought Amanda's stuff inside. I wasn't trying to make her leave me alone. I was trying to bring her back. Not just the whistling wind that had carried her voice, but my sister, the person I'd fought with, shared a house with, all my life. She wasn't coming back, though, not now, not ever. I knew that, had known from the day they threw cold dirt over her grave, six long months ago.

I wasn't like Mom and Dad, hoping some baby would take Amanda's place. I knew that my sister was dead. I *knew*. What was wrong with me?

My head hurt, and my hands started to shake. I suddenly needed to get out of there. I ran from Amanda's room and slammed the door shut behind me, ran through the house, ran out the front door. I jumped on my bicycle and pedaled hard, needing to go as far and as fast as I could. I rode until sweat plastered my shirt to my back, until every muscle in my legs ached. The heat rose as morning gave way to afternoon, making the air swim in front of me, but I didn't care. I didn't think I would ever be warm enough again.

When I finally did return home, though, the cool air inside felt good against my hot skin. At first I assumed the air conditioner was running, but then I remembered I'd turned it off. I glanced down the hall, toward Amanda's door. It was open. Had the cold in her room somehow seeped out into the rest of the house?

I swallowed hard. I remembered closing Amanda's door, too.

For a while I just stood there, clenching and unclenching my hands. Maybe wind had blown the door open. Maybe the latch hadn't caught properly. There were lots of reasons the door could be open.

And I didn't believe any of them. I knew what I did believe, knew I was crazy for believing it. I took a deep breath, walked down the hall, and stepped through the open door.

Amanda sat on the edge of her bed, just like I'd hoped—been afraid to hope—she would.

Her face was pale, her dark hair limp around her shoulders, but otherwise she looked perfectly healthy, like she had before the first time she'd gone into the hospital. She stared down at her blue quilt, as if she'd never seen it before.

She'd come back. She really had. My stomach lurched. I thought I might cry, or throw up, or start laughing and never stop. Instead I flew across the room to grab her into a hug.

My arms passed right through her, through empty air; I stumbled and nearly fell onto the bed. A clammy shiver raced down my spine. Amanda didn't even glance up. I stepped back and looked at her harder. Her body shimmered, very slightly, and through her I could just barely see the bedroom wall. I reached my hand out more slowly. It passed straight through Amanda, through air cold as winter, cold as the snow that had been falling the day she died.

A ghost. Amanda was a ghost. What else had I expected her to be? I drew my hand back, touched it to my face. The hand was icy cold. I shoved it deep into my pocket, trying to warm it.

Amanda still hadn't noticed me. She reached down toward the bedspread, trying to lift one corner of it. Her hand passed right through, too. She took a deep breath, and a chill breeze crossed the room, carrying the bedspread toward her. She let the breath out, and the blanket fell limply back to the bed.

She looked up, as if realizing for the first time I was there. "Brenda," she said, her voice strange and low.

"Amanda." I shoved my other hand into my other pocket, feeling suddenly uncomfortable. We stared at each other in awkward silence, as if all those years of fighting hung in the air between us, and neither of us knew what to do.

Amanda looked slowly around the room, at all the books and posters, then back to me again. I saw cold, glittery tears in her dark eyes.

"It's not fair," she said.

I just stared at her, still unable to speak. Of course it wasn't fair. Unfair that she had gotten so sick, with nothing anyone could do about it. Unfair that the house was so weird and empty now. Unfair that Amanda wasn't around anymore, to fight with and grow up with, and maybe one day figure out how to get along with.

"It's not fair!" Amanda said again, louder this time. Her eyes turned bright and angry. "I just want to hang out with my friends, and watch TV, and go to school, and be normal, you know? I'm not ready to die of some weird disease most kids haven't heard of and I can't even pronounce. I don't want to just give everything up."

My throat felt suddenly dry. I swallowed. "At least you have your room back," I said. That was something, wasn't it? It was what Amanda had wanted.

"I don't care about my stupid old room!" Amanda's voice rose. Bright tears trickled down her cheeks. Wind whistled through the room, knocking a row of her own books off the shelves. "I want it to have never happened! I want someone to tell me they made a mistake!"

"Me, too," I said. Amanda blurred in front of me, and I knew my own eyes were filling with tears.

Without warning, the wind died. Amanda wiped one hand across her face and looked straight at me. "What do you mean, you, too?" She sounded surprised. "I thought you just wanted my room and my stuff and all. I thought you'd be glad to get rid of me."

"No!" All of a sudden I was the one crying, choking on my words. "No, Amanda. What makes you think I'd want your things instead of you? Don't be stupid!"

"I'm not the one being stupid!" Amanda shouted, a flicker of the old challenge in her eyes. But then she sighed, and the flicker died, and I knew that I wouldn't even get to fight with her again, any more than I'd get to do anything else with her again.

"I didn't want to lose you," I said. "I never wanted that."

Amanda sighed. Cool wind fluttered through the room. "You mean it?" she asked.

I nodded. "Of course I do."

Mom told me once that fighting doesn't matter so much when sisters get older. I didn't know, would never get to know. My stomach twisted, harder than before. Like Amanda said—it wasn't fair.

Amanda closed her eyes. For a long time she was silent, and when she opened her eyes again, they held a strange, almost peaceful, look. "It isn't fair," she repeated softly, as if somehow reading my thoughts. "But there's nothing we can do."

Her quiet words bothered me more than all her yelling, more than her throwing stuff around the room. I didn't want her to accept this.

If she did, I'd have to start accepting it, too.

I wanted to argue, to tell her she was wrong, that there must be something we could do after all, something all the doctors had somehow overlooked. But there was no point in fighting now, because for once Amanda was right.

I could still see through her, more clearly than before. She was slowly fading, the room growing warmer as she did.

I reached out toward my sister. She reached back. For just a moment I felt the warm clasp of her hand in my own. Then that, too, began to fade.

"You can have my stuff if you want," Amanda whispered. "I guess I'd rather you have it than anyone else. You, or maybe the new baby." Her voice turned still lower, so low I strained to hear. "You know, once that baby comes, you'll be the older sister. Try to do a better job than I did, okay?"

I wanted to tell her that she hadn't done a bad job, that she'd just been there and been my sister, and what else was she supposed to do? But even as I opened my mouth, her features blurred, turning her to little more than a shadow. The shadow faded, then all at once disappeared.

Leaving me standing in my bedroom, alone.

Who knows what evil lurks in the heart of the wood?

THE SHADOW WOOD

Sean Stewart

Once upon a time there was a kingdom whose name no man remembers. The people of that country and their King were very proud, for their land was a rich one. Fields of grain covered the prairies of the west, fishermen came back with full holds from the eastern sea, and the cattle and horses of the north were the envy of the world.

But the King got nothing from the forest of the South, for it was cursed. Many ages before, a great darkness had been prisoned there, in what men called the Shadow Wood. But as time passed, the people forgot why they had been warned against entering the forest. Folk began to remark on how much richer they all would be if the Wood could be chopped down for its lumber, and fields planted in its place.

Finally the King was convinced. "The whole

world envies our eastern seas, our western prairies, our bounteous north. And yet they laugh at us because we will not master the Shadow Wood. This is intolerable!" So he summoned his army and bade a hundred men go into the Shadow Wood and claim it for him. His armorers fitted them with spears and shields, and his priests blessed them with prayers and incantations, and the people of the capital rejoiced.

On a morning bright with sunshine the hundred men set out. The smell of them was of fresh oil and leather and high resolve. The sound of them was of young men singing, fearless and full of joy. The sight of them was of brave steel and pennants snapping in the breeze.

But the hundred men marched under the shadow of the Wood, and they did not come back.

So the King sent out two hundred more to look for them, but they did not come back.

And the King sent forth five hundred after them, but they did not come back.

Then the King sent ten hundred men to find those who were lost, but they, too, vanished and were never seen again. Joy left the kingdom, and silence came upon the armorers and the priests and the citizens of the capital.

"So it is," said the King at last. "We are not meant to have the Shadow Wood. Let that be an end to it."

But the next day a young hero came to the

capital. He bore on his face the triple scars of a master of the Hundred Schools of Combat; a long-handled steel dangled at his side. Its edge was as keen as the north wind, its hafts were shaped like two feathers, in honor of the Gull Warrior, and in the pommel of the blade sat one of the precious blood-red gems that only swordsmen who had learned the Way of Stone were permitted to bear.

The young man came to the palace in the morning and was granted an audience that very afternoon. "I see you are a student of that long-handled steel," the King said. "You bear the marks of the Hundred Schools, the Way of Stone, and the Gull Warrior, too. What brings you to my court?"

"I am a hero by trade," the young man said. "But I need to make a name for myself. I have heard of the men you lost in the Shadow Wood. I intend to venture there myself, claim the forest in your name, and find the men who went before. If they are alive, I will rescue them. If they are dead, I can at least see they are decently buried, and perhaps bring back a keepsake or two for their grieving widows."

The King said, "You may dare the Wood if you wish—but I cannot recommend the enterprise, for the rate of return has not been good."

But the young man, who was much more brave than wise, said, "It was not I who went before," and hastened from the room.

Now he meant to plunge straight into the forest, but as he left the audience chamber a wrinkled hand plucked at his sleeve. The wrinkled hand was attached to a withered arm, and the withered arm led to the spindly body of an old man. "Tarry a moment, young hero."

"I am afraid that is impossible, wizened ancient. I am off this very instant to explore the Shadow Wood."

"This I know," the old man said. "And I applaud your audacity!"

Now, this particular old man was not nearly so brave as the young hero, but he was a great deal more wise. He also knew more about shadows, and darkness, and the cursed Wood than was altogether proper. Had the young man looked carefully into his eyes, he might have seen enough to make even him afraid.

But the young man did not understand that some dangers cannot be vanquished by a stout sword arm, and paying close attention to men with muscles smaller than his own was not in his nature. "Do not try to stay me with counsels of cowardice, wrinkled sage. My heart is set on this adventure."

"And credit it does you!" the old man exclaimed. "Listen but a moment further." (Now, it is a curious fact that with even a little experience it is possible to lie as easily as one tells the truth. Some people even find it easier.) "I lost a brother—a brother very close to me—to that evil Wood many years ago, but my heart tells me he lives yet. If you see him, will you rescue him from the shadows?"

"But of course I will save your brother!" the young man said. "What else would a hero do?"

A corner of the old man's mouth twitched as if he meant to smile. "O most excellent youth! Let me grant you one thing more to help you in your quest, that you may surely bring my brother back." The old man burrowed in a pocket and brought out a little silver box with one match inside and a tiny candle made of golden wax. "Only this. It is not much, but when all else fails, light the candle and you will see an answer to your problem."

"Many thanks, feeble grandfather!" With a deep bow and an elaborate flourish the young man took his leave and headed for the city's southern gate, and the dark Wood beyond.

He followed the way the soldiers had gone, far, far into the forest, until slowly the footprints became confused. The broad track branched, and branched again into dozens of tiny crooked paths. At first he tried to follow always the largest path. When all had shrunk to little more than deer runs threading between the trees, he wished he had kept a more careful memory of his choices. In truth he was not certain of how to get out of the Wood again. Not that he was afraid—there was no challenge under the eaves of this forest, he was sure, that he could not meet with his long-handled steel.

It was dark in the forest, though. The leaves that stirred as he passed seemed to whisper to themselves. The branches closed behind his back. Back in the capital he had taken the little golden candle mostly to please the old man, but out here, in the darkness, he was glad of the thought of its flame.

Late in the afternoon he felt the ground shake as if afraid and heard the sound of a great beast moving through the Wood. Vast trees parted like grass before it, and it walked with a mountain's tread. The young hero was tempted to use the golden candle and see what magic the old man had sent to save him, but instead he drew his long-handled steel and turned to face an enormous wolf with limbs of rock and a muzzle of iron, towering taller than the tallest tree.

They fought until sunset, but the young man knew the way of the Gull Warrior, who cuts and melts and is not struck, and at last he conquered his foe.

The next day found him hungry and cold and tired from the battle. He had brought a loaf of bread and a wheel of cheese and a skin of water with him. As he ate, he found himself hoping that he would soon come to the heart of the Wood and discover the fate of the King's soldiers. He did not wish to spend too long here, he realized. Just long enough to make his name and his fortune.

That morning, as the young man strode through a clearing, he happened to kick over an anthill. As if at one signal, the ground around him heaved and quivered, and a torrent of giant ants rose from it, each the size of a wildcat. Again he thought of the golden candle, but instead he gripped his long-handled steel and fought for his life. All morning the battle raged, and all afternoon, too, and the young man was worried and circled and chittered at by a thousand foes. But he knew the Way of Stone, that stands even before a thousand waves and is not moved, and when the setting sun ran like blood from a wound between the mountains of the west, the last ant was vanquished. The young man threw himself on the ground to sleep, ringed by a wall of his dead.

The moon had died in the dark before dawn when he was awakened by a mad gibbering that filled him with dread. *This would be a good time for that golden candle,* he thought, but it was dark, and he could not remember where last he had put the precious thing. The gibbering grew madder, and louder, and finally the young man whirled, snatching up his sword. He found himself beset by a headless champion dressed in slate gray leather, wielding a terrible weapon: for this dark warrior used his own head as the ball of his mace.

"We do not have to fight," the young man said.

The mouth gaped. "It is my nature."

"I warn you, I am a master of this long-handled steel."

"No, you are its creature," the mace said. "You are merely a weapon, as am I. The difference is, I know who is wielding me." And with that he struck.

They fought a terrible battle from dawn to dusk. The forest rang with the clash of steel. But the young man knew the Hundred Schools, and at last the groaning mace fell silent.

When the final blow was struck, the hero hung gasping over the hilt of his sword. But only after he found the little golden candle and put it in a pocket just above his heart did he throw himself on the ground beside the headless champion. There he slept for a night and a day.

When at last he woke, he decided to strike for home. "I have wandered here for three days while the paths have grown smaller and smaller. Perhaps the Wood has no heart. Perhaps it is only paths and darkness, and the bodies of the King's soldiers lie hidden forever under roots and leaves, and if I do not turn back now, I, too, will be lost. I have slain the Wood's guardians. That should be enough."

In fact, he was lost already. His last battle had carried him away from any track. By day

he could see no paths, and by night the stars were hidden. He grew thin with hunger and dry with thirst. Finally, the evening after he had eaten his last crust of bread and swallowed his last sip of water, he spied a light. With a cry of joy he followed it, arriving at last at a great house carved from the flesh of scores of standing trees. Gleams of lamplight slipped out from under the leafscreen like sly glimpses from hooded eyes.

Boldly the young man strode forward and knocked on the front door, a vast portal carved in a hollow trunk. The sound of his knocks boomed within the tree, fading slowly like the sound of a stone dropped in a deep well.

The door swung open. An old man stood behind it. Our hero started back in surprise. "By my long-handled steel!" he swore. "You must be the brother of the withered sage I met in the capital! Two men could not look more alike. I could almost think you were the same man, brought hither by some strange enchantment."

"You don't say?" One corner of the old man's mouth twitched, as if he meant to smile. "Be that as it may. You must be cold and weary, for the forest is dark and full of peril. Will you not come in?" And he held the yawning door wide.

For one long moment the young hero paused, reluctant to cross the threshold. *Am I to quail now?* he rebuked himself. *I who slew the wolf with limbs of stone, and the mound of ants, and the headless champion? As long as I have my long-handled steel, what harm can come to me?*

With this thought in his heart he meant to stride forward, but his legs would not move. Only when he put his hand on the pocket just above his heart, and felt the silver box there, and the little golden candle, did he draw a deep breath and step inside.

"It is very dark in here," he said.

"You will get used to it, in time."

The old man began to climb a flight of steps carved into the tree's heart. These led up a great distance to a walkway between two trees. "So! You made it here. Few travel even one way through the Shadow Wood. Did you then fail to find its dangers?"

"With this long-handled steel I conquered the worst the Wood had to offer."

The old man laughed. "Oh, not the *very* worst, I don't think."

Darkness whispered between the branches. As they walked from tree to tree, the planks creaked and swayed beneath their feet.

"Tell me, doddering wise man, how did you come this far into the Shadow Wood?"

The old man had reached a door in another vast tree. He turned back and gave the hero a long, curious look. "It is a great truth, one very hard to learn, that old men were young once.

And it is even harder," he said, "for a young man to grasp that someday he, too, will be old."

Leaves whispered.

"When I was your age, I, too, was a great adventurer," the old man continued. "I won through to this place with my wits and a piece of steel with a handle just the length of your own."

"Then why are you still here? Surely a man who survived such perils could not lack the resolve to leave the forest?"

The old man had gone ahead, and his voice carried weirdly through the echoing gloom. "Who, me?" he said with a strange little laugh. "Oh, I am a terrible coward. Why, I am afraid of my own shadow!"

"This will be your room," the old man said. The bed's curving headboard rested against the north wall of a hollowed tree; high on the south side a window notch flooded the guest room with moonlight. A curving staircase wound up through the middle of the floor, vanishing into the ceiling.

"I shall only trouble you for a single night," the young man said. "Tomorrow I will be fresh again, and with your directions we should have little difficulty leaving this melancholy forest behind. Of course I will take you with me."

"Do you think so?" the old man said. "I think, sometimes, that a man never truly leaves the Wood, once he has strayed here. I wonder, sometimes, if even the capital is not merely a clearing between the trees. A kingdom has its borders, don't you know. But the Wood gets into your heart. You carry it with you, wherever you go."

"You speak in riddles," the young hero said. "I only know I do not like the darkness. I like to be able to see my way clear before me. I long to be out on the plains and in the sun!"

The old man said, "Just so. Pardon my fancies. Well, I shall be in the room below. Good night, and good luck!"

With this unsettling remark he vanished down the stair, and the young man prepared to sleep. His every muscle burned and his every bone ached. His skin was a tapestry of bruises. He wanted nothing more than to crawl beneath the covers of his bed and snore the night away.

And yet he could not sleep.

The forest was in his room. The silken pillow felt like moss beneath his ear. The cloth coverlet felt like softest heather on his body; it smelled of wet leaves and blood and vixen. Outside, the secret trees whispered and bowed, and shadows crept around the corners of the room, rising and falling, slipping away at the edge of sight.

What had the old man said? He was afraid of his own shadow.

The young man found himself staring into the darkness, flinching at every creak of the wooden floor or crack of the wooden ceiling. He had the strangest feeling that his very essence was bleeding slowly from his pores, swirling out to the room's edge to be consumed by shadows.

Nonsense, he told himself. They were shadows, nothing more. Shadows couldn't hurt him.

He found his hands were shaking.

A muffled cry from the room below made him leap to his feet. Grabbing his long-handled steel, he rushed down the spiral stairs.

The old man's bed was empty. Quivering like an arrow in a target, the young man stood on the lowest stair, eyes wide and fixed on the creeping night. He saw nothing but moonlight and dim shapes and the shadows of tree limbs, crossing like ancient hands rubbed together in sinister amusement. Finally he stepped toward the bed, walking like a dancer on the balls of his feet.

For a long moment he stood motionless beside the bed. Then with a great cry he flung back the coverlet. The old man was gone. But underneath the blanket, hard-edged in the moonlight, lay his shadow.

The young man yelled and ran for the stairs. A flood of shadows poured after him. When he reached his own room, he risked a quick glance back, but the moonlight showed the horrible truth: The shadows were following him. Somehow he knew that once drowned beneath that tide of darkness he, too, would never leave the darkling Wood.

Up he raced, and up still farther, until he thought his heart would burst, pounding up stair after stair until he found himself in a tiny room with no more stairs to climb. It creaked, that treetop room, swaying in the murmuring wind, and the floor sloped this way, then that.

He was desperate. He could flee no farther, but neither could he cut the darkness with his long-handled steel. Then, at his wit's end, he remembered the candle.

With shaking fingers he plucked the silver box from the pocket of his shirt, shook out the single match, and struck it on the bottom of his boot. He blinked in its sudden light and then held it to the tip of the tiny golden candle.

The candle spat and sparkled into life. The young hero set it in the middle of the floor and then whirled with a great cry as the first shadow slid up the stairwell behind him. The young man lunged, jumping before the candle flame, and then struck into thin air.

The shadow hissed and writhed and died—for now the young man had a fine shadow, too, and a long-handled darkness to wield against the night.

He stood against the shadows like a stone, lanced through their ranks like the Warrior, and then melted away. He needed every trick he had learned from the Hundred Schools, for against him were ranged the shadows of the one hundred men the King had sent into the forest, and behind them the two hundred, and behind them the five hundred, and the thousand sent to search for the others.

But the young man was strong, and swift, and in the end the last shadow, stooped and wizened like an old man, turned and fled down the stairs. Curiously, this final shade rubbed his hands together, and the sound of the wind hissing through the branches outside was like the sound of distant laughter.

The young hero laughed, too, for he was brave and a champion, and now he had surely conquered the Shadow Wood. Then he leaned upon his hilts, spent in every limb, and watched the golden candlelight sparkle down the length of his long-handled steel. He had turned back the tide. He was alone.

Almost. There was still a silver moon and a dark Wood outside. The wind still whispered, and a wild scent like wet leaves and vixen lay heavy in the air.

The young man glanced up at an unexpected movement. His eyes widened as a dark shape rose and walked across the room.

His shadow, his own shadow leaned forward, glancing up at its master. And then, with the mallest, softest sigh, *it blew the little golden dle out.*

from deep within the darkness, the ughed.

ABOUT THE AUTHORS

AL SARRANTONIO's short stories have appeared in magazines such as *Twilight Zone* and anthologies like *The Year's Best Horror Stories*. His stories and novels span the science fiction, fantasy, horror, and Western genres. He and his family live in New York's Hudson Valley.

ANN S. MANHEIMER has been a camp counselor, a child care worker, a a journalist, and a lawyer. Now she lives with two daughters, her spouse, and two black cats in a house overlooking the San Francisco Bay. She writes stories and wishes she knew more algebra.

MICHAEL AND ROZALYN MANSFIELD are an artist-writer team who create fiction and educational materials. They live on an experimental organic farm in Huntsville, Texas, where they grow giant pumpkins and other unusual plants with their daughter, Ilyana.

ANDREW (A.J.) FRY is a sixth-grade student in the Talented and Gifted Program at Shelton View Elementary. He lives with his parents and younger brother Corey in Seattle, Washington. A.J. enjoys soccer, writing, and art. This is his first published piece, hopefully of many!

MICHAEL STEARNS grew up in San Diego, where as a boy he traded baseball cards with a professional knife-thrower. He writes stories and has edited three anthologies of young adult fiction: *A Wizard's Dozen, A Starfarer's Dozen,* and *A Nightmare's Dozen*. "Gone to Pieces" is his first story for younger readers.

GREG COX has written several books, including *Star Trek: The Next Generation: Dragon's Honor* and *Iron Man: The Armor Trap*, and has had stories in anthologies like *The Ultimate Spider-Man* and *Alien Pregnant by Elvis*.

PATRICK BONE is a professional storyteller who writes poetry, songs, and fiction for children and adults such as the picture book/audio, *There's a Dead Boy in the Attic and Other Strange Stories*. He lives in Tennessee, in an old house adjacent to a small cemetery.

[illegible] LEE SIMNER grew up on Long Island and [illegible] in Tucson, Arizona. She's published [illegible] in nearly two dozen magazines and anthologies—including *A Starfarer's Dozen* and several books in this series—and is the author of the *Phantom Rider* novels.

TIM WAGGONER has published stories in anthologies like *A Horror a Day: 365 Scary Stories* and *100 Vicious Little Vampire Stories,* and magazines like *Mythic Circle* and *Thin Ice.*

JOAN AIKEN was born in Rye, Sussex, England. She's written over fifty books for children and adults, and received honors such as the Guardian Award for Children's Literature. She and husband Julius Goldstein divide their time between homes in Sussex and New York.

SEAN STEWART was born in Texas but raised in Canada. His first novel, *Passion Play,* was named the Best Canadian Science Fiction novel of 1992; his second, *Nobody's Son,* won for 1993 and was named Canada's best young adult novel for the year.

JOHN PIERARD has illustrated all the books in this series, as well as the *My Teacher Is an Alien* quartet, and the popular *My Babysitter Is a Vampire* series. He lives in New York City.

Photo: Jules

BRUCE COVILLE was born and raised in a rural area of central New York, where he spent his youth dodging cows and chores and letting his imagination get out of hand. He first fell under the spell of writing when he was in sixth grade and his teacher gave the class an extended period of time to work on a short story.

Sixteen years later—after stints as a toymaker, a gravedigger, and an elementary school teacher—he published *The Foolish Giant*, a picture book illustrated by his wife and frequent collaborator, Katherine Coville. Since then Bruce has published more than fifty books for young readers, including the popular *My Teacher Is an Alien* series. He has long been fascinated by the art and science of fear, and thinks that nightmares can be fun, as long as they stay in your head where they belong and don't start crawling out of your ears and causing *real* trouble.

These days Bruce and Katherine live in an old brick house in Syracuse with their youngest child, Adam; their cats Spike, Thunder, and Ozma; and the Mighty Thor, an exceedingly exuberant Norwegian elkhound.